I0555646

SELF-MADE WIDOW

Also by Philip Race

Killer Take All

As E.M. Parsons

The Easy Gun
Fargo
Texas Heller

SELF-MADE WIDOW

PHILIP RACE

CUTTING EDGE

Copyright © 1958 by Philip Race

The characters and events portrayed in this book are fictitious. Any similarity
to real persons, living or dead, is coincidental and not intended by the author.

No part of this book may be reproduced, or stored in a
retrieval system, or transmitted in any form or by any means,
electronic, mechanical, photocopying, recording, or otherwise,
without express written permission of the publisher.

ISBN-13: 978-1-952138-15-7

Published by
Cutting Edge Publishing
PO Box 8212
Calabasas, CA 91372

CHAPTER ONE

Don't tell me about failure. I wrote the formula, and I know every damn trick of the trade. The sly ways of not admitting it; the methods whereby you arrive at someone else's responsibility for your actions—the whole bit. And the ways you make up for it, oh brother! Beat your wife, take a running jump into a bottle of konk—or leave a monument to weakness by taking your own life.

Or somebody else's.

And that's murder.

We had onions for supper. Tiny ivory-white onions, the ones you find on the bottom of cocktail glasses. It seemed to me we'd been having the same meal pretty often lately.

"It's not your fault, Johnny," Edna said. She swished her glass. "Bellotte isn't half the man you are. But he's ruthless, and you're too soft for your own good."

"Let it alone, Edna. He got the job. I'm still the war hero with a pretty smile and not much brains." I twisted in the deep chair, set my empty glass on the low coffee table that separated me from my wife. "He said I'd missed too many days. Made too many sales contracts in bars. Christ! How do they expect you to sell the lousy stuff—in church socials?"

I tried to keep the bitterness out but it came through. Edna leaned forward, her perfect face concerned and dark with anger at the machinations of business.

"Darling, you mustn't let them use you. That's all they're doing. Can't you see that? Who got the Navy contract? And that big one with the overseas construction outfit? Why, they must be mad."

"Let it alone, Edna."

"No, Johnny. You've done that long enough." She leaned forward, the front of her dressing gown falling open, exposing the tops of swelling breasts. Even now, half-drunk and hissing with the cold disappointment of losing the sales managership I'd thought was mine, my wife's beauty excited me. Four years hadn't changed that. "No, Johnny. You've got to see that you'll never make it far in that business. Because you're too good, too worried about other people. And you can't be that way. You have to scratch. You have to kick, not worry about hurting others. Then when a crack opens up in front you dash through."

"Dash," I said. The radio switched from music to a news broadcast and I turned the volume way down. Warm California night washed through the open French doors. "Dash is for sprinters. I'm built for distance."

She didn't smile. Her eyes were focused somewhere out in the suburban dark; her fingers idly rolled the onion which she'd fished from her drink. I watched her, throat tightening. God, she was beautiful! I'd never ceased to wonder at the fact that she was mine. It had been the uniform, probably, and the ribbons. Korea had still been a fresh memory and even statuesque chorus beauties read the papers.

She popped the onion into her mouth, wrinkled her nose at me. "You're staring."

I started to get up, go to her. The drinks got to me. Those we'd had for supper and those I'd solaced myself with all day since finding out about the promotion I didn't get. My head felt thick suddenly. I fell back in the chair, covered my eyes with my hands.

"Darling, what's wrong? Are you sick?"

Edna's arms slid around my neck. I shook my head against her. She held me, murmuring and petting. Only some strange core of pride, holding out against the alcohol, kept me from blubbering like a baby.

It was always like that. Edna kind and loving, willing to find excuses for my shortcomings. She was fire in velvet and fever in silk, a body that men stared hungrily after in a market or on the beach. But she was mine.

And it was I who always failed.

I pushed her away, finally, got unsteadily to my feet. Her face, a pale circle in the low light, looked up at me. I walked to the small bar I'd spent four week ends building. She said nothing, but sat quietly, eyes following me constantly. She never said anything when I came up short. That hurt me, I think, more than anything. Edna deserved more. Much more. Not West Anniversary Drive and a slowly disintegrating husband who owed everybody, drank too much, didn't sell enough steel any more to justify his desk. I tried to shrug off these things. But it became increasingly more easy to stop in at the York Club after work, pick up a dram or two. Some nights I didn't get home at all.

It was half-living and Edna was caught in it—a slowly creeping horror that we couldn't fight, couldn't really see.

The bottle I was holding tipped a glass and I cursed without spirit. Edna walked up behind me.

"Me, too," she said. "Make it strong. We'll celebrate anyway, darling. Just as if you had got the job. It's their loss. What do we care?"

Her hands touched me: I froze there, eyes closing.

"Don't let it get you, Johnny. We're all right. We've got each other. ..."

I spun away from her, clenched my hands at my sides. I wanted to hit her and it frightened me. Her eyes widened and her hand went to her throat.

"Johnny, what's—"

"Shut up! Don't say anything. Don't sympathize." I wiped a hand across my eyes. "Why don't you scream and rant like other wives? Why don't you tell me you're bored silly with this stupid life and this funny house? Why don't you throw things and curse and tell me about all the other guys you could have married?"

I stopped, breathing hard. The soft music from the radio echoed in my head like an out-of-tune boiler factory. Edna stood without speaking. Her face was soft. Even now, when my attack was direct, my rage bent inward and exploded upon what I loved most. She folded her hands in front of her, lifted her chin. The eyes were calm and unblinking.

"I'm your wife, Johnny. What you feel, I feel. What you want, I want, too."

And she meant it. I was sure of it. There was a quiet intensity about her words, a passive honesty.

She turned suddenly, strode to the window, hips swaying under loose silk. She looked outdoors, spoke quietly. "We can't go on like this. Not anymore. I'm happy just being with you, Johnny. But something's happened to you, something bad. You're eaten up inside and sometimes it's hard for me to recognize the man I loved and married."

"Edna, listen." I started towards her, stopped when I felt my head begin to swim again. "Not for me, Edna. You mustn't ever think that. What I want, I want for you. Nice things, time to enjoy them. Now, while we're young, while there's still time. If it hadn't been for the war…"

She turned. "We wouldn't have met," she finished.

One hand held the drape over her head and the slender, rounded body drooped against the window casing. It drew my gaze like flame a moth.

"Sit down, darling. I'll make the drink. We won't talk about it anymore."

I moved to the chair, flopped. My eyes hurt and I rubbed them. Often I've wondered what impulses lead a man to take his own life. I could never figure any reason big enough. Now I got the first suspicion of how easy it would be. What had I ever done for Edna, my wife, my mate? What prompted a vivid woman to waste her life with a slob like Johnny Babcock?

Glass tinkled in the room; the soft night silence deepened by contrast. I dropped my head into my hands. Edna's voice came from near at hand; she stood close beside me, looking down.

"There has to be more than this, Johnny. You want nice things for me. Well, all right. So do I. But I can wait. I have confidence in you, darling. You'll be given a chance someday and then you'll be big. We've had some bad breaks, all right. A couple of badly timed sicknesses. Certainly not your fault."

I said, "Sicknesses! I was sick, all right. Johnny Walker sick and ninety proof diseased!"

"Johnny, honey … everything will be fine." Her hand touched my head, slid down to my neck. I could feel the silk against my arm and I gripped her robe, hid my face against her.

She began to cry. For the first time since we'd been married, Edna cried. I broke away, stared incredulously.

"I can't stand seeing you like this. I can't!" She crossed her arms over her breasts and hugged them. "Johnny, I'm half crazy. … we've got to do something."

"Edna, don't. Please don't. I'll—get another job. Yes, that's it. My experience, my record. I'll go somewhere else—"

She stopped my lips with her hand, smiling now through the sudden tears. "No, John. It's too late to start from the bottom again." She flattened her palms on either side of my face, lifted it. "You don't like this job. You never have, really. You kept it because of me. Because it brought enough money to keep us comfortable, to live decently. But that isn't enough, I guess. And that's my fault. I should have been strong enough to make you go on with your music. To take the lean years and bet that your talent would catch a brass ring for both of us."

She was wrong, so wrong. But I hadn't the guts to try to make her see it. The Army had ruined any chance I might have had of becoming a concert artist. It hadn't been Edna that drove me back to the green sanctuary of Donaldson-Rhine.

"All right," I said, more to myself than her. I'd finally made up my mind. If being the All-American boy wouldn't do it, then I knew a way that would.

"What, honey?"

"Edna, do you remember the plan?" My voice was flat, dull. She drew in her breath sharply.

"For real, Johnny?"

"For real."

The radio murmured; I switched it off. Edna stood twisting her hands. Outside, a cicada rasped its nightly exercise. A horn sounded far away, carrying on the night air.

"Do you know what you're saying?"

I nodded, leaned back and closed my burning eyes. "I know. I know I'm through bucking all the odds, going up against a stacked deck. Through eating crow and smiling stupid smiles at vicious little people in high positions. Through. Finished. Just damned sick and through!"

I head the whisper of silk as she walked, smelled the dark musk of her perfume. Against my closed lids red pictures scrambled like technicolor time exposures on murky film.

I spoke very quietly: "We'll both wind up bent and old, darling. Used up. Still reaching for a dream that just doesn't seem to be in the cards." My voice dropped. "We've talked about it often enough. Now we'll do it."

I sat up, picked up the drink she'd placed beside me. I didn't look at her; my eyes stared without focus, feeling like two leaden eggs floating in acid.

"It was just a joke, Johnny. Never for real."

"Now it's for real."

And just like that, it was done.

Edna sat on the edge of the coffee table, took both of my hands. "You know what you're doing, Johnny? What you're committing us to?"

I nodded, unable to speak. Something flashed deep in her eyes, was gone in an instant.

"Then that's the way it'll be," she said.

I reached for her blindly and she came into my lap, held me tightly. We kissed; she tangled one hand in my hair and met my mouth with hers open, demanding. It was a long kiss. Not like four years married—like four days, four minutes. Finally we lay huddled together in the chair, breathing like one organism, shutting out the world and first-of-me-month bills and a thousand petty defeats.

And the horribly growing, howling thought that somebody we didn't even know would die.

The beginning. We had played with our little plan, talked about it, laughed over possibilities—the more fantastic, the better. You know, like people do. Honey, if we had a million, well, we could burn down the house, collect the insurance. One thing leading to another. A joke. Ha, ha. But the money really would be nice. Oh, yes.

The Plan. We lived in it, now. Thrived on it. I found myself drinking less, finding it possible to face the slobs with their sly grins about me missing out on the job of sales manager. I could meet the smiling hypocrites without the confidence of morning sips, and constant recharges. I had a new, deeper confidence now. I could smile at them.

How do you rationalize murder? Does the reasonable explanation—and you've got to have one—just leap full-blown to mind?

Or does it slide piece by piece into your leaden consciousness, fall glibly from your lips when conscience gnaws?

"Johnny, don't think about it, don't worry about it and don't moralize. If it's what you want to do then do it, and the world be damned!"

It was easy for Edna. She was part of me; what I did, she shared. But the spreading sickness was my own.

My job suffered after our little joke had become a plan. Not much, because for months I'd been walking through the thing, perfunctory and contemptuous. Edna was good; never a word that her man contemplated a crime. Just a smiling acceptance and a tight-lipped calm against my moods, my fears. And surprisingly, when we discussed the details of murder, she thought of things with her clearer mind that I might have forgotten.

I was looking for a man to kill.

I FOUND HIM. It took a week but that was all right because there were other details to work out. He had to look a little like me, you see. Just generally, build and age. This one did, I made no contact. I wasn't ready for that yet. But I had seen him, marked him. He would do. ...

That night I drove home in the Ford, threading slowly through the evening traffic. I knew the moment I told Edna about the man there'd be no turning back.

One hundred thousand dollars is a lot of money. It will buy so much, more perhaps than a man has to sell.

The house was dark. Edna met me in the deep shadow of the porch, eyes gleaming in the semi-dark. Her chestnut hair caught every spark, every vagrant sliver of light, turning it into copper magic. She wore an ankle-length hostess gown slit almost to the thigh. Green, very tight. A smooth knee peeked through the slit.

"You're late, Johnny."

I leaped the steps, dropped the briefcase to the porch. My arms swallowed her and she came against me for an instant.

Then she pulled away, turned her lips from my kiss. "Hey," I said. "What's with you tonight?"

"Nothing, darling ... it's just—"

She broke off, glided across the porch to lean on the railing. Her hair moved with the slight breeze.

"I can't stand this strain any longer, Johnny. I guess that's it. I can't, I'm sorry, but I can't. It's unnatural. Whatever we're going to do, we've got to do soon."

I moved behind her, close without touching. The night got small and dark, extending no farther than the edge of our green-clipped square of yard. She said one word and it hung there while the whole of both our lives sharpened, came together and crystallized in that instant.

"When?" she said.

My hands went around her filled with her fullness.

"Any time you say," I whispered. My lips ran down her neck, nuzzled the cool hollow of her shoulder. "Any time at all."

She whimpered and turned inside my arms. Her head bumped my nose, lifted. Her lips were leaping pads of warm velvet and her body trembled under my hands like a buzzing fluorescent tube.

"I'm glad," she breathed, when the kiss was done. "No more waiting and wondering. I'm glad."

She held me off at arms' length. The silk gown rode up and down with her breathing, sliding like shadow over the curved mounds of her breasts.

"Now we go," I said.

She nodded. "You found a man. Tell me about it."

Not knowing why, I moved away, trailing my hand along the rough railing. I looked at the dark. A sprinkler whirred somewhere, forgotten.

"Nothing to tell. I saw a guy. I can find him again. He might do."

"He'll do, Johnny. Something's got to break right for once. Oh darling…" She ran to me, plastered herself to my body. Her eyes were slits of silver between silken lids. "A hundred thousand dollars! All the money in the world. No more short end of the stick, no worrying about whether some idiot likes you enough to give you a five-dollar raise. People and places, sweetheart. Clothes, excitement. All the—"

She stopped suddenly. I guess I was looking at her curiously. Her arms dropped; she lowered her eyes.

"Just—just tell me what to do, Johnny. Don't let me make a mistake that'll hurt you."

We went inside. Edna got away quickly, bustled in the kitchen. I fiddled with the television. Nothing on but crime stories. I flipped it off and lay back in my chair. For a while the thoughts whirled around; then I fell deeply and dreamlessly asleep.

Edna woke me hours later. I was hungry. My clothes were sweat-soaked. I smiled sleepily at my wife, ran stiff fingers through snarled hair.

"Hi, babe."

"Hi, guy." She smiled, but it was a forced little smile. The strain was telling on her, all right. I'd have to go ahead now. She pushed a drink into my hand. It was cold and sharp, with just enough gin.

"Sandwiches," she said, pointing. She reached out a hand, brushed the hair back from my forehead. "My poor darling. I'll make it all up to you. I promise."

I nodded, drained the drink.

"Okay, kid. School's over." I straightened in the chair, pulled my rumpled clothes into shape. "Now we get down to business. If we want to stay alive."

"All right, Johnny. You talk, I'll listen."

I motioned for another drink. She poured my glass full from the frosted shaker. I bit into a sandwich, put it down.

"You know what we're doing, what we're getting into. It's dangerous. Real dangerous. Especially when the insurance people start growling."

Edna lit cigarettes for both of us, puffed daintily.

"Every little thing becomes important now. We're playing with lives. Our lives. The police can blunder all over the place. For them there's no penalty for failure. But us—well, we can't afford to miss. Not once. The tiniest mistake and we're dead. You understand?"

"I understand." Her hands lay open on her thighs, palms up. She was more controlled than I.

"First, the insurance company investigators. They're good. They'll be nosing around. That's where the test will come. You can bet they'll be hot-nosing until the company's completely satisfied."

"You don't think they'll be satisfied?"

"I know damned well they won't. Not a week after issuing a new policy. Just remember—"

Don't worry about that." She sipped at her drink. set it carefully on the gleaming surface of the coffee table. "If you do what you must do, I can certainly carry out my part. I'll get the money."

I nodded. "Right. I'll do the—"

My voice stopped in my throat. Right then I felt a foretaste of disaster; it slimed my tongue and chilled my body. I got up abruptly, walked to the window. A paper match crumpled in my fingers as I tried to light a cigarette. The striking strip eluded me and when I did get the damned match lit, I couldn't hit the end of my cigarette. I dropped both to the floor, spitting out the butt.

I turned, said, "Christ!" barely whispering it. "It scares hell out of you, doesn't it?"

Edna nodded, eyes bright with a suspicion of tears. "I've been scared before, Johnny. Scared that I wouldn't get out of that shack where I was born ugly, that I'd never live at all. And most of all—" she got up, stood with her head down, not looking at me— "scared that you wouldn't marry me. How could he want me, I said? A leg-waver, a chorus cutie. After that, nothing can be bad for me again."

I reached her in a rush and buried my face in her hair. Her hands held, caressed. Inside I was shaking like suet pudding.

"How," I whispered, "how did I ever get a woman like you?"

She pulled back, smiled slowly with her eyes, hot now, caressing my face. Her hips leaned into me, moved gently. She leaned forward and her warm lips opened like a split plum.

CHAPTER TWO

There is a park in the heart of the city. Not much of a park—walks in the form of a giant X; a pavilion, raised a little from ground level; brass between the walks. One city block. Later the ranters against fate and government would be out in force, destroying the city's serenity, rattling dust from the leaves of the ratty palms. Now, only sleeping men owned the park.

The sun had dried the short-cropped grass and the air was warm. There was a faint odor of flowers sifting through the exhaust fumes and rubber smell. The lawn was dotted with shabby men lying in grotesque positions, eyes shaded by newspapers or disreputable hats. Some clutched paper bags or dirty parcels.

It was hot for me wearing a suit and hat. The briefcase weighed a ton. I walked quickly to where my man had been the first time I'd seen him. And there he was. I took off my hat, sat down beside him on the browning grass. No one paid any attention to me at all. He slept on.

He was a tall man, like me; thin, with a dirty black stubble covering gaunt cheeks and prominent jaws. An ancient felt hat, which may have been almost any color once, shadowed the upper part of his face. The hat was stained and misshapen, as was the brown suit whose lapels had been turned up around the man's neck and fastened with a safety pin. His shoes were a flapping-soled disgrace.

A real mess, this kid. I touched his shoulder; shook him several times.

"Hey, buddy. Hey, there—"

He cringed away from my hand, rolled. Then he straightened on one elbow, blinking. His eyes were almost entirely shot with red, the lines spidering out from shriveled pupils of pale, pale blue.

"Awright, awright," said the man. "I'm going. Gimme a minute. I'll be awright in a minute." His voice was fuzzy; the words ran together oddly.

"You don't have to get up. I'm not a policeman."

He looked at me, blinked several times while the words searched for meaning in his fuddled brain.

"No cop?" He sat up all the way, the beginnings of anger in the slant of the stubbled jaw. "Then what's the idea? What's your goddam story, mister?"

"No story. You uh—you hungry?"

"Sure, I'm hungry. I'm always hungry. What's it to you?"

"Nothing, really. Just curious."

"What I really need's a drink." He worked noisily at clearing his throat, spat far out on the grass. "That's what I really need." He rubbed a trembling hand over his lips.

"All right." I got a bill out of my pocket, passed it to him. "Here's a buck."

"What for?" he asked, but he snatched it, looked around quickly at the other sleepers.

"Wake-up. If that's what you need. You ought to eat, though. You really should. You're thinner—" I got up on my haunches— "thinner than I am."

The bill disappeared into the pinned-together front of the brown coat.

"No strings?"

"No strings. Get some soup, though."

"Oh, yeah—sure, you bet."

He stumbled erect and stood weaving slightly. I rose quickly beside him. My size, all right—tall and thin; shoulders broad and a little bowed; big, knobby joints. Close enough. Nobody would ever recognize him, anyway. He'd be Johnny Babcock. We walked out of the park together, down sixth street.

"You coming to see how I spend your buck?" he asked, as we fought the noon crowd on Spring street.

I just shook my head. The street was busy; cars crawled bumper to bumper in sullen lines, reflections in the polished sides distorting the sidewalk crowds.

"You're wondering, I guess, about me."

"Not especially," he said. "You want to give away money, why I'm the man'll take it."

"I mean, well, why should I give you a buck? Or anything. What's my story, as you said."

"All right. What is it? You a Christer?"

"No. Not a do-gooder." I dodged a militantly striding woman loaded with packages, caught up with my derelict. He was moving, too. Wine in sight. "Just curious, you know? Impulse, I guess. There I was, walking through the park, and I thought I'd find out something. Something I've wondered about for years. You know—what makes you people... you, uh—"

He laughed a short and ugly laugh, phlegm rattling in his throat. He hawked and spit into the gutter. "You mean winos, huh? You wondered why we guzzle? Don't worry about nothing but the next bottle?"

"Yes. That's it exactly." I smiled a little guiltily—and I wasn't entirely acting. "I work in an office—salesman. Same thing every day. A guy wonders..."

"Nah," the ragged man said, not bothering to look at me. "That ain't it, champ. You got a hatchet. Everyone's got a hatchet." He shrugged. "But I don't care. What can you do to me?"

What, indeed? The plan all but exploded right there. But I laughed—hollowly, I'm sure—and said, "Hatchet? I don't know what you mean."

"Yeah, to grind. You know, axe to grind? What's in it for me—that bit?"

"No. Not me. No axe. You got any people here? Here in the city, I mean."

He stopped suddenly and I walked past him a few steps. When I turned he faced me, loose features tight now, grown solid with suspicion.

"How much you think you buy for a buck, champ?" He fumbled in the ruined coat. "Here. You take this crap and rub it in your hair."

"Wait. Look, I'm sorry." I pushed the money back at him. "No more questions."

We started walking again. I'd have to forget about the background, take a chance. I stopped him at the corner of Main. Traffic rushed by in a heedless stream.

"This is where I get off. Got to work. Before I go, how'd you like to make twenty bucks?"

"Twenty bucks? Well, look, mister—like, I'm a bum, maybe. But I'm no crook, see?"

"Oh, no. Nothing crooked. Strictly legitimate. Are you interested or not?"

"Sure I'm interested. If it's legal. That County Jail is no bargain. What do I have to do?"

"Nothing hard. Work, but not hard work. I got a little cabin—"

"Oh, wait a minute. Work, now…"

"Nothing heavy…"

"I been sick, mister."

"Nothing to it. Needs a little cleaning. The cabin. Screens—you know. Not too much. I'm pretty handy. Need a little help, is all."

"I been sick. No kidding."

"Twenty bucks…"

"Yeah, but I don't know. Work, now…"

I shrugged elaborately. "Okay. Thought you could use the twenty is all. I'll get someone. So long." I started off. "Get something to eat, huh …"

"Well, wait a minute. Don't run off, now." He pushed a hand into the small of his back. "My back is …" He really needed that money. Or thought he did. I watched greed struggle with laziness. Finally he sighed and nodded, averted his eyes like he'd agreed to officiate at an autopsy.

"Nothing heavy, mind?"

"Nothing heavy," I agreed. "Meet me by the stone lions in the park. You know, the statues on the east side? One o'clock right on."

"One o'clock tomorrow. I'll be there."

"No. Not tomorrow. Saturday. My day off. I have to work tomorrow."

He nodded, taken with the idea now. "I'll be there, mister." He shuffled a step away, came back. "How about an advance? A little one?"

"Like how much?"

"Oh. five—" He looked at my eyes— "two, maybe. You name it."

I handed him a five dollar bill. He grinned, shook his head from side to side. "You must be a Christer. Like I figured."

What could I say? He was happy and full of the easy money in his pocket. So I just stood there and he started off, dodging in and out of foot traffic, in the direction of the teeming skid row section just down the street. It was Fifth street and I didn't look at it very closely.

I should have.

A hard lump materialized in my stomach, just under my rib cage. For no reason.

I called after my derelict: "Hey!"

He stopped, turned. Passersby looked at me strangely. I waved. "Saturday," I called.

He waved in return and disappeared into the crowd, moving rapidly toward his reason for living.

I didn't even know his name.

A secretary ushered me into the oak-paneled office in the Mercury-Consolidated building, with a polite murmur that Mr. Freese was expecting me. I'd socked down three doubles after the encounter with the man in the park and my ears buzzed, not pleasantly. The lump was still with me.

The room was big and finely furnished, with a polished free-form desk set smack in front of a nearly wall sized picture window. The window was the big feature of the room—except for its occupant, Albert Freese. Over fifty, he wore a shantung suit and made it look good. He had a lamp tan and the rough wrinkles of lots of years in insurance. He greeted me, sat me down and we had the weather and baseball bit until I wanted to spill the desk over on him.

Finally, I said, "Could we get to the policy, please? I have another appointment."

Freese broke off an observation about somebody's batting average and shifted gears smoothly.

"Of course." He pressed a buzzer, straightened. "Preliminaries all in order. Doctor's report, credit report. Ah, so. Matter of a signature. And the initial premium. Pretty big policy, Mr. Babcock."

"I know. I've got a check right here."

The secretary came in with some papers; she carried a notary seal in a chamois bag. She spread the documents.

"Before we close, Mr. Babcock," Freese said, "I'd like to level with you."

"About what?" I moved forward in the chair. "Don't you want to sell me this policy?"

"Yes, I suppose so. It's a good sale. Young man, healthy. Fifty thousand life … double indemnity clause. But we investigate. And in your case I made it through." He racked back in the tan swivel chair, looked at me from under bushy, gray brows. "Understand? Here's our position. Expensive plan, bought by a young man of modest means. Big premiums. No immediate return in sight. Why?"

"You trying to talk me out of it, Mr. Freese?"

He sighed. "No. That's not up to me. Something about it bothers me. Don't know why. Good local family. School here, then U.C.L.A. War record, an asset. Married four years. Seven years with Donaldson-Rhine, counting the war years. But—"

"But what, Freese?"

"Nothing I can touch. Just talk. Office talk. Drinking, missing work—things like that. It's a pattern. After a few years in this racket you recognize them. Plus an expensive wife …"

I looked hard out the window at the high building, the city far below. A perfect day, smogless and clear as a stream; a high glare of pale sunshine through which bits of dust danced in the uprush of air from the squirming streets. The park was out there, just below.

Freese sat considering me with eyes almost closed. slumped in his chair.

I said, "Can we sign?"

He roused. "Yes. Might as well." He took a pen from an onyx holder, held it out to me. "Where you see the X."

I signed. The secretary, mute and neat, did the seal business. Freese scribbled a receipt, blotted it expertly and handed it to me along with the thick fold of engraved bond that was my copy of the policy. I handed him the check.

I could leave then, and I did. My first stop was a bar, the York Club, two doors from the Mercury-Consolidated main entrance.

It was a business men's bar, narrow, neat, and low-lighted, abounding with charcoal suits and thin ties. The talk was a mutter of prices and campaigns. It competed with a tinkling Tatum-style piano from the juke box. Maybe Quincy Jones. I found a stool near the deep end of the bar, sat and ordered a double Johnny Walker. I couldn't go home. Not now. That was a mortal cinch.

The drink came and I put it away. It went down like water. Warm water. Question: How much scotch does it take to wash down murder? The man poured and I experimented.

CHAPTER THREE

The girl came in about four. Three-thirty or four. The air in the joint was hazy, full of drifting tendrils of smoke; the same music insinuated through the small talk. Except now I knew who the piano was—Theolonius Monk. I'd deposited a flock of dimes to make sure the music didn't stop. The tunes were bluesy and wonderfully articulated and suited my mood exactly—complicated and lowdown. By that time I had reached the brooding stage, twiddling my glass and glowering at the back mirror.

"Hi." It was a little voice, but warm.

I turned, saw a pretty, heart-shaped face, smiling nicely, a trim body perched on the edge of the next stool. I blinked. The girl widened the smile and the outside corners of her eyes tilted upward. She looked very nice, very neat.

She leaned toward me, making a face. "You're loaded," she said.

"I'm loaded."

A wave of good perfume, not too heavy, floated up from between her breasts.

"Are you too loaded?" she asked, leaning again.

"Too loaded to what?"

"Why, for a matinee, honey." She cocked her head to one side. "Interested?"

For just a minute I had no idea what she was talking about. Then I looked at her with new interest. She sat erect on the stool, almost prim, in a jersey thing that looked to be tan or beige. You couldn't tell for sure in that light. Her hair was brown, too, and appeared soft, with highlights in it.

"You want a drink, miss?"

She turned from a sober contemplation of her face in the bar mirror. The smile was gone. Her face was composed and cool; the only life a faint sparkle in the up-tilted eyes.

"Drinking's not my business, handsome. Do we or don't we? It's that easy."

The bartender hovered, sweating noticeably in the midday heat. The girl's hands twisted in her lap. She said nothing so I ordered. Scotch for me, Martini for her. I shook a cigarette loose, offered it to the girl. My hand wasn't very steady. She considered me for a moment, eyes washing over my features slowly, cataloguing them. She took a cigarette.

"You're in fine shape, kid," she said, bending toward the match I held.

"I'm fine. You got a name?"

"Dee," she said, expelling smoke.

"Just Dee?"

"That's not enough? You want a number, maybe?"

"No, no. That's fine." I turned to the bartender, paid for the drinks. "My name is Babcock. Johnny Babcock."

"Johnny?"

"I'm a salesman," I explained, feeling I should.

"Well, now that's real nice, Johnny." The girl sipped her Martini. "You want to go to my place this afternoon, Johnny? Or what's this little act all about? You're not all that drunk."

I picked up the Scotch, put it down again. The buzzing was louder, now. A pleasant, light sensation crept up on me. The girl's influence—and Johnny Walker. She said something. The girl, not Johnny Walker.

"Humh? You say something?"

"Again," she said, depositing her empty glass on the wet bartop. "You want to turn a trick with me?"

"Sure," I said, grinned at her. "You bet. How about another drink first?"

"Look. I told you, buster—"

"Bartender! Two more here." I turned to her. "For the road. Don't be so serious. Life is real, life is earnest."

I worked a little at my smile and got one in return, a nice one. Not at all like a hustler's smile. She said, "Something in there about an empty dream, too—isn't there?"

"I don't know. Maybe. 'S a long time ago." My eyes followed the firm curve of her breast down over gently flaring hips to the bent thigh, full and womanly. The jersey hugged her flesh. I looked up and met her eyes, peering over a rounded arm.

"All right?"

"Umh. Nice. Very."

She hesitated, eyes on mine. Her closed look melted for an instant. Then she turned to her drink, a faint flush darkening the clear skin at her cheeks. That seemed odd. I hadn't known many whores, except in the service, but those I had come in contact with hadn't been like this one at all. This Dee.

"I guess maybe I did want a drink." She spoke straight ahead, without looking at me.

I fiddled with my own drink, said nothing. The silence was not uncomfortable. The mirror was gold in tone and it softened detail, flattered. In it I watched the hollows in the girl's throat as she drained the martini glass. Edna was more classically beautiful—features pure, cleanly cut, emphasized by perfect coloring. But there was something about this girl—

There it was. Sooner or later all women must be compared to Edna. By me. The girl, Dee, found my eyes in the mirror. We sat like that for quite some time, just looking, saying nothing. Finally, she finished a drink—the fourth, or maybe the fifth—and turned to me. Her rounded knees were held together, hands laid lightly on the swelling thighs. She had an air of not exactly unpleasant exasperation.

"Look," she said. "You're nice. Real nice. But I've got a living to make. This kind of thing makes for bad dreams. And right now is my busy time. It's almost six o'clock. This is my busy time."

"You said that."

"I know. Now, don't—"

"Listen," I said. "I told you I'd turn—what was it you called it?"

My cheeks grew hot and she saw it because she laughed. A short, tinkling laugh, abruptly stilled. As if she hadn't had much practice lately.

"Turn a trick, honey," she whispered. Her fingers slid inside my arm, gripped lightly. "What do they call it in your circles?"

"Marriage," I said. I slugged down a drink, covered her fingers with my big ones. Hers were smooth, stubby and well cared for, with square-cut nails innocent of polish. "You ever been married, Dee?"

"Now, wait a minute—"

"No. I'm siserous—serious. I mean it." I blinked at her, wet my lips. "What I mean is, why is it so hard? How come something's always happening to tie up your guts?"

The girl drew back from my whisky breath, tried to pull her hand away. "Easy, buster. Cool it, now. What are you trying to prove?"

"No, listen, kid. I did all right in school. you know. Football and studies and everything. I made it in the service, lots of decisions. Made 'em all right. But a simple little thing like making a living, I'm fourteen thumbs and a vacuum skull. And Edna never—well, never mind that."

I twisted on the stool until our knees touched. The girl's eyes were wary, now, withdrawn. She thought I was nuts and maybe she was right.

She said slowly, "Wife trouble, huh?"

"No," I said. "No, it's not that, exactly. But—"

"It's all right, Johnny. That's how I make my living." She smiled, the slant eyes pushing up. "That's why I play the business district. You'd be surprised how much action a sharp gal can pick up in the afternoon. A guy stops for a few slugs, he isn't in too much of a hurry to get home."

"That isn't what I mean," I said. My hand fumbled for a cigarette, brushed the briefcase on the bar. The policy was inside and suddenly I was sure everyone in the bar knew what I was carrying in the tan holder. "But let it go. I don't know what the hell I do mean. Tell me about you. You don't care about my funny old problems. You always work around here? The financial district?"

The girl's face changed. "We have to talk about me?"

She jerked away from my hand, turned back to the bar and drained her drink. Her lips had slackened a bit; the fast Martinis were getting to her. She dropped her gaze to the bar-top, spoke low: "Give me a cigarette. I'm getting silly or something."

"Or something," I said. Just to be saying it.

The bartender came up, waited. I gave him an order, turned back to Dee with two cigarettes lit. She was picking at the dress where it swooped between her thighs. Just picking, picking. I lifted her chin with a finger, put a cigarette between her lips. Her eyes were shadowed again.

"You're very good-looking," she said, for no reason that I could see.

"That's hard to believe."

"Why?"

I shrugged. "My wife," I said. "She's a—well, you'd have to know Edna."

"That her name—Edna?"

"Yeah. And she's beautiful. Really beautiful, like no woman ever should be. So damned cool and tall and if you don't watch out I won't let you look at me. Aah..."

I revolved the stool, looked for my glass. The mirror shimmered like a golden pool, caught my eyes. For a moment I forgot to drink, forgot Edna. The mirror went in and out, in and out. Dee's face, concerned and very young suddenly, moved in and out of focus with the mirror's reflection.

"Why do you hustle, Dee?" I said it, then thought about it. My ears grew hot and I couldn't look at her. She didn't answer for a moment; it seemed very still though the bar sounds went on. "You don't have to answer, of course. I'm not sure why I asked."

"It's all right." Her voice was low, contained. "You're all alike—the nice ones. All alike. Wanting to know how such a sweet girl got to be a whore."

"Dee…"

"No," she said, turning toward me. "Don't feel badly. That's the way it is. There's no profit in calling a spade anything but what it is."

"But nobody has a right to hurt another person. For just nothing. Just to be hurting. And that's what I—"

"Shhh," she said, and attended her drink.

I sat there, waiting. I couldn't stop her now—she was primed. She folded her arms on the bartop, leaned over them, body inclined from the waist. Her eyes followed streaks of light in the moisture from the glasses.

"Johnny, I haven't been a bum very long. Not nearly long enough to get as hard as you really should be. It's a tough life. And it's new enough to me to hurt when someone—some clean, nice guy like you, reminds me." She took a breath, fiddled with her purse on the bar. "Most of the stories are the same. Little different dialogue, maybe. Always a man and his lies and eventual disillusionment. I used to think it was too corny. And it is corny. The only thing is, it happens and when it hits home it isn't corny any more. It's dirty, and rotten luck, and unkind fate—and any other excuses you can think of. Mine's no different. Except it happened on an arty plane."

She sniffed audibly. I signaled the bartender, dropped a bill on the bar. My last Scotch was still untouched. Now I sipped it.

"That's a laugh, isn't it? Arty. But that's what happened. I was taking drama at the University of Chicago and they picked me to do the annual play. I was a big star. Cicero style. And then, this guy—" Dee dropped her forehead onto the fingers of one hand, rubbed lightly— "Frank was his name. Quite a guy."

I pushed my drink around on the bartop. She chewed her lip, looking inward. The reflection of what she saw there warped the fresh firmness of her face, fuzzed the sharp outlines.

"He came backstage that night," she said, still not looking at me. "Told me about his connections in Hollywood, dropped names all over the place. I was nineteen. And he was well-dressed and very good looking."

"How old are you now?"

"Twenty-one." She roused, downed a brimful Martini and pushed the glass aside. "You know anything about women, Johnny? No, of course you don't. Nobody does. It's the damnedest thing. First love. The world in a bucket and rose-colored glasses that won't quit. Everything sings, you know? I hadn't been exposed to much charm. Not the practiced kind pimps use." She looked up at me obliquely, then looked back at the wet circles on the wood. "Frank was my first big love. The first I—"

I put a hand on hers, squeezed. She worked up a crooked smile.

"Still hurts, I guess."

"Sure it does. Don't talk about it. I'm sorry I asked."

She went on, as if I hadn't spoken. "I would have done anything for him. Anything at all. He was a fascinating bastard."

"Most of them are," I said. The bartender caught my eye and I motioned for more drinks, shoved a bill out.

Dee said, "Yes, I guess they are. But for me it was the grand romance. The big passion, like they write about. It bothered me a little that he wouldn't marry me. But I figured, what the hell,

I've got Frank. I had him, all right. For two weeks until we got to California."

The drinks came and we each sipped. I lit cigarettes. I could think of nothing to say to her. Dee let her cigarette burn between her fingers, stared at the curling smoke. Some fool played a rock 'n roll record and the sound washed over us and around us and somehow we were all alone at the crowded bar, welded by a strange sharing that neither of us could have defined or explained.

"So there I was in California, land of promise. Boy, did I get promises! The honeymoon was over but I was too dumb to know it. I remember the night Frank told me I'd have to go to work. Sleep with strange men for money." Her voice stayed even, low and matter-of-fact. And that heightened the ugliness, the dirty little bits of lives, that came through her story. "I fought with him, unbelieving. Then I tried to kill myself. Oh, not very hard. I really didn't want to die. I just wanted Frank to say, 'There, there, darling; I was joking.' But he wasn't and he didn't. They pumped out the silly pills and Frank took me home, got me drunk the same night. That's the night I turned my first trick. Sloppy drunk and sure the world had ended."

The cigarette had burned down almost to her fingers. I reached over, took it away from her. She didn't seem to notice. The bartender hovered and I waved him away.

"After that it didn't matter much," Dee said. Her fingers intertwined on the bar and one thumb monotonously rubbed the other. "I kept getting drunk and I kept on turning tricks. But the bloom was really gone, now. I didn't even have my great love to sustain me. Frank made me sick. Physically sick. I couldn't hide it and he beat me for it. When he did that, I ran away. My folks sent me some money and I stayed drunk for a month. I don't remember much what happened. One day I woke up and realized what I was doing to myself. Twenty years old and already defeated and used. Maybe if I'd met a guy right then—some nice, steady, ordinary type guy with no ideas louder than half an acre and four kids."

She shook her head, swirling the short hair. Her eyes turned to me and they were wide and murky, clouded by sick memory. She tried a smile but it just wouldn't come.

"That was the time to go home, Dee. Back to your family, your friends."

"Maybe," she said. Her hand sought the small purse, got out a handkerchief. She used it quickly, crumpled it in her hand. "I sobered up, anyway. Dee, I said, you came for a career. So make like an actress. For a while there I thought I had it made, too. I got a job, saved money. Went to drama school and found out how much I didn't know. Then I set out to capture the theatrical world. Frank was just a bad dream. One mistake didn't mean I had to give up."

She laughed. Short and hard, coughed up out of the heat in her throat.

"The first day I was registered at Central Casting I got four calls. Three from guys in the industry who remembered me for night dates. And one to make a dirty picture." She sighed. "Well, that tore it. I dove back into the bottle and when I came up again I faced it."

She twisted on the stool, took a big breath. "Confessional, huh?"

I could say nothing; I drank.

"So here I am," she said. The tilted eyes swept up in a mirthless smile. They were wet at the corners. "And thank you, Father Babcock."

"The hell with it, Dee. The hell with all of it."

I slammed around on the stool, angrier than I could ever remember being and not having the least idea why. I banged on the bar and hollered for the barman, spat words at him when he arrived. Dee put a hand on my arm.

"Come on, guy. It's not all that big." She smiled for real, although a little sadly. "All I stopped for was to see if you wanted a matinee."

"Look, it's none of my business," I said harshly. My head was thick and cottony, thoughts tangled. "None at all. Me playing father confessor. That's the biggest laugh."

The briefcase lay there on the bar-top, slick and leather-shiny, innocent and ordinary. I picked up a drink, spilled most of it before I got it to my lips. I didn't even feel it going down.

Dee said, "You hear me, Johnny? I asked if you still wanted to—" She stopped, her eyebrows drew together, twin lines of curved shadow. Her eyes slid a little out of focus. "What's wrong with me?" she whispered.

"Dee. If I want to see you again, if there's a time we can talk, maybe…"

She straightened. "Yes. Now I've got to go. You ask the bell captain at the Thessaly Hotel. He'll know where to find me. His name in Julius."

"Julius at the Thessaly," I repeated numbly.

She gathered her tiny purse, turned.

"Wait!" I caught her arm. "Don't leave. I'm—Look, Dee—" I pulled her head around, looked into the gray eyes. "I need you. Right now. To talk to. Please don't go."

"Johnny, I—" She pulled on my wrist, got loose. "See Julius at the Thessaly. I've got to go now."

"One more drink," I urged.

Over her shoulder I saw two men in business suits stop to watch our actions. Then I forgot them. Dee stood, head down, trying to extricate her wrist from my new grip. The top of her head came only to my chin. The juke box quit. Just like that, the joint was a tomb. No talk, no tinkle—no nothing.

"All right, break this thing up." A tall guy with a bumpy face and narrow shoulders stepped between us. He wrapped long fingers around Dee's arm, pulled her aside. "We'll take care of her, buddy," he said to me.

"Hey, wait," I said. "What is this?"

I slid off the stool. My knees almost buckled; Scotch fumes rose in my throat.

"Easy, Mac," the other man said. He was a carbon of the first; neat suit, white shirt, clean shave—but heavier, wider in the shoulders.

"Wait, now," I said, trying to be reasonable. "What's the idea, here?"

"We been trying to nail this broad for a month," the skinny one said. He flipped a wallet open with his free hand, not letting go of Dee. An LAPD buzzer flashed in the bar-gloom. "She hasn't been working the financial beat long, but she's a smart little broad."

Dee looked up just enough to see my eyes. Her lips were drawn, the color having fled. She shook her head shortly.

"Just a minute, now." I said. The whisky zoomed and I cursed myself for loading up. "You're making a mistake here, officers."

"No mistake," the first cop said. He pulled Dee's handbag from her fingers, felt it expertly for weapons. "This's the broad, all right. You won't have to sign a complaint or anything, so don't worry."

"No. You don't understand. This is my wife."

I said it and fell into a hot silence like a whisky bottle into a church service. Dee's head snapped up and she tried to take a step forward. The cop jerked at her and I took a step toward him. The wide one stopped me with a thick arm.

"What'd you say, Mac?" He moved forward truculently.

"I said, take your hands off my wife. So we have a little argument? So whose business is that? Turn her loose, God damn it!"

The heavy cop shouldered me back, bent an elbow across my chest, pushing me back over the stool I'd just vacated. My back hit the bar. I didn't move.

"This guy could be her pimp," Heavy-shoulders said. His swarthy face was right on top of mine and his eyes were nasty. "Turn around," he barked.

I smiled right into his dentistry. Maybe it wasn't a very successful smile, but it must have been honest. Or something. He hesitated in the face of it, anyway, then stepped back, glowering. I straightened, tugged my coat around.

The thin cop asked the bartender: "You know this guy?"

"He comes in."

"This his wife?"

"Well, now I don't think so. But—"

"You're laying yourself open to something," I said, butting in. "All of you. You better check this—" I fumbled in my pocket, got out my wallet. "When you finish, get your hands off my wife. And apologize to her, or God damn me if I don't sue the brass right off your buttons!"

The cop took the leather, scowled at me. The identification was solid. Why not? Hadn't I spent thirty years establishing Johnny Babcock? The cop checked everything, holding the cards up to the light. Sheriff's card—that was a dilly, Donaldson-Rhine Credit Union Certification of rating, Diner's Club card—the whole bit. It was solid, all right. Even a Screen Actor's Guild card I'd gotten during college while working in a picture one long-gone summer. A football picture, I remembered inconsequentially. The cop pulled them all from the wallet, held them, fondled them, scowling all the while. He turned to the bartender who had come around to our side of the bar.

"You're Harrison?"

The man bobbed his head, wrung his apron. "Yes, sir. Robert Harrison. I own this place. I called you, sir. You see this—"

"I know," the tall cop said, cutting him off. "This broad—" he grinned at me— "this broad the one you told us about?"

The other patrons had drawn close, drawn by the excitement. I recognized a man I knew—Charley Dawson, an executive of a firm I did business with. He looked at me and asked a question with his eyes. I gestured to him, turned to the cop.

"...you see," Robert Harrison was saying. "And when she said that, well, I called you fellas. Like you told me. And that's what she said: You gonna turn a trick with me, or not?" His eyes touched me, slid away. Sweat beaded his bald head. "That's what she said," he mumbled.

"Officer..."

He turned to me. "Look, mister. We know what you've trying to do. Maybe we even appreciate it a little. But we've got a job to do. What do you care about a little tramp like this one? She was ready to take your dough, wasn't she?"

"I told you, she's my wife. This man here—" I pulled Charley Dawson into the circle— "knows me. We do business together. He can vouch for me."

"I know him, all right," Charley said.

The cops stopped, turned their attention to Dawson. He was a fat boil in a three-hundred dollar suit, groomed and pink from good food and massages. He looked like money, and he was money.

And he knew Edna.

His eyes, milky and suspicious, probed mine, hunting for a clue.

"And he knows my wife," I said, stepping forward. "Tell them, Charley. How long have you known me?"

He rubbed a fat finger alongside his nose. His lips twitched the merest trifle. "Long time," he said. "Been doing business with this boy ever since he came back from Europe with all those medals for bravery." That was a nice touch. He pulled his wallet from an inside coat pocket. "I'm C. W. Dawson. Dawson Roller Bearings—Shell building."

"See," I said. Charley never had said that Dee was my wife. I tried to stampede matters and pulled her away from the cop's grasp. His fingers had left red marks on her smooth arm. "Now, suppose you apologize..."

"Just a minute," Bumpy Face said. "Let's not run away, here." He held up one of my cards—driver's license. "You live at this address?"

I nodded and the cop turned to Charley.

"You been to his place, Mr. Dawson?" A note of respect had crept into this tone.

Charley frowned. The ground was safe. Or should have been. He had visited me once. But I wasn't sure he'd remember where the house was. He bit his lip, looked up.

"Sure. West Anniversary, isn't it, Johnny? Or East, or something. That's close, I'm sure. I can't remember the number."

The cop grunted. Nobody spoke. A compressor hummed.

"Could I have my wallet?"

The heavy cop leaned against the bar and looked at the three of us—Charley, Dee and I—with an odd, long-suffering expression on his bumpy face. He said nothing. Then, after a long, scowling moment, he said: "Let's go, Morry. The broad has no record. We'd have trouble. We been had."

They turned together, still a team, and started off. The bartender raised his hand, like a boy in school. His face was streaming sweat.

"Officer," he said. "Aren't you going to—"

"Drop dead," the one called Morry said.

"Hey," I called. "How about the apology?"

Dee dug an elbow into my ribs, moved against me. Even at that public moment I was conscious of the firm length of her nestling in the crook of my arm. The vice-squadders turned at the door.

"Don't push your luck, kid," the heavy one said wearily. "Just thank God you were known." He jerked his chin at Dee. "'By, baby. We'll see you later, I'm sure."

They went out.

Charley turned. His eyes glistened and his huge belly shook with repressed mirth. He held up a hand. "No, Johnny. Don't tell me about it. It's more fun this way. Maybe you can do something for me."

I nodded. Too full of something—I didn't know what—to speak. Dee thanked him. She did it very nicely. She reached out and held both his hands and looked him full in the face.

"Thank you, Charley," she whispered, eyes misty, body trim and erect. "Not for helping—but for what you just said."

He cleared his throat, looked over her shining head at me. He gave a little shrug. I'd known Charley Dawson for years. But until that moment, I hadn't really known him at all.

"Can I give you kids a lift somewhere?"

"No, Charley. And my thanks, too." I got my briefcase from the bar. I'd almost forgotten it and when I hefted it, it weighed a ton. There were some bills beside it. I picked them up, left the change. The bartender sidled up, wiped hesitantly, avoiding my eyes. He looked at the money, made no move to take it.

"You're a swell guy," I said, conversationally.

I pushed the silver at him.

"Look, mister, this is my place. And I got a license. You know? I got to keep it."

"Nice guy," I said and pushed the handful of change over the edge of the bar, into the station behind.

The dropping sound was loud in the quiet. The man's face flushed. Dee gripped my arm.

She said, "Don't forget that he's right, Johnny. He is right, you know."

He was, and she was. We got out of there.

Charley left us at the street and Dee and I walked for a long time without speaking. It wasn't bad with her, not speaking. It felt comfortable and full. Her hand rested inside my arm; once in a while I'd look at her, catch her looking at me, eyes big, the tilt at the corners slightly accentuated by the shadows. It was dark and getting chilly. She had no coat and all I had was my suit. I stopped by a white-lighted beanery on Spring Street.

She turned, looked full into my face, said nothing.

"Hey," I said, grinning down. "Anybody home?"

The white face was like wax. She looked, gaze unblinking, eyes traveling all over my face, my hair. Then she grabbed me and pulled my lips down to hers in a cruel, hard kiss.

She pulled away, finally. "I have to go, Johnny. Right now."

"Wait, now. I thought we had an appointment." I grinned at her, fought for balance. "Why do you think I saved you?"

What makes a man do things like that? Dee crouched a little, drawing a breath that should have burst her lungs. Her eyes filled quickly like holes in the sand, and she seemed to sag. While I searched for something to say, she left. I heard her heels tapping on concrete, almost running, going away.

"Dee…" I said "Wait…"

But I didn't mean it. The lump was back under my rib cage and the briefcase again weighed its true ton. And Edna waited in a funny little stucco house on West Anniversary Drive.

CHAPTER FOUR

West Anniversary Drive is a long, curving street of private homes, branching off from a paved arterial connecting with Ventura Boulevard. There are streetlights on the corners; none in between. Most of the houses are one story, California ranch or Spanish modern. All have small squares of lawn in fronts and patios in back.

They seem very much alike in the darkness. Especially when you're walking and drunker than a roomful of actors.

I stumbled along the sidewalk, clutching the briefcase, searching each house I passed for a clue. I'd recognize mine, of course. But then I hadn't been able to find the Ford. It was somewhere downtown. Or in Hollywood. Or Gardena. I'd made them all after the scene on the street with the girl. A taxi had dropped me at the corner and now I trudged in the weak moonlight, cursing without spirit at the unlighted porches.

It was late. Very late. All of the good, solid, mow-the-lawn-on-Saturday suburbanites long in their righteous beds. I sneered at the thought and it made me belch. Scotch fumes rose in my brain and I stumbled. The street was longer than time.

Then I saw the light. My house, my light. Streaming through the French doors on the side of the house. I wasn't even on the right side of the street. I stood on weaving legs in front of the house, looking upward at the pale moon riding slickly between scudding, smoky clouds. Somehow through all the drinking and what-all, I had kept a tight hold on the briefcase. The air cleared my head a bit, and the thought of Edna inside waiting helped, too. I walked across the lawn.

She didn't look up as I entered. The radio played softly beside her chair, tuned to one of the all night record programs. Her nails were freshly polished; bottles of gunk sat here and there, and the smell of banana oil filled the room. It didn't go at all well with the Scotch.

"Hello, Johnny," she said, straining to be reasonable.

Her skin was flushed and I could see she wanted to explode, to do all of the things I'd always told her she should do. She didn't, of course. She wouldn't have been Edna if she had. "You're very late," she said. She cocked her hand, blew on the wet nails.

I said nothing, my tongue thick. Her legs were drawn under her on the deep chair. She slid them out, flashing smooth thigh. She flowed upward, stood with her head thrown back looking at me. Just looking. Her lips moved. "Poor Johnny."

"Edna…"

She whirled suddenly, walked quickly to the window, laid her forehead against the pane. She spoke from that position, the words muffled but audible.

"Johnny, we can't do this. I sat here for seven hours. Seven hours. What's gone wrong, I thought? Did the insurance company get suspicious? Maybe he tried to run, got hurt."

"Edna, listen." My tongue finally came unstuck. "I got the— Everything's all right, baby. Believe me. I got the policy. Right here. And I found the man."

She turned slowly, looked at me with narrowed eyes. Tiny white lines etched the corners of her mouth. How much could I pain this woman? How many times would she be here when I'd stumbled in my own sick despair?

She said, "All right, darling. Get cleaned up. We'll talk about it."

She brushed by me, patted my cheek. She went to the big chair, sat wearily. Seven hours. I could see the effects. And Edna wasn't strong. She was fine and delicate and I knew myself for a fool!

I moved toward her, moving carefully, like a man carrying nitroglycerin in an open glass. Some idiot on the radio promised a rich, full life in a newly opened sub-division called Day-in-the-Sun Acres.

I bent over, very gingerly placed the briefcase in her lap, on the silken thighs. She looked at it, not moving.

"Open it."

Her fingers played with the catch. The whisky came up in me again and the room dipped. I stumbled out, almost running.

It took about an hour for me to run a tub, soak and begin feeling almost human again. I toweled off, rubbing hard, and brushed my teeth, though it almost killed me. The gums were sore from alcohol and bile. I wrapped a robe around my nakedness and joined her.

She was reading the policy.

"There it is," I said, uselessly.

"Johnny," she said. "I knew you'd do it. I knew it, darling." She held the paper against her cheek and smiled up at me. Her tongue ran along her lips. "Come here."

I reached the chair in a stride and scooped her up, spilling the manicure paraphernalia all over. Her arms went around my neck, one hand clutching the policy.

The bedroom was dark and I left it that way. One square of pale light from the high moon stretched across the bed. A charge had come into the air; the outside sounds were swallowed in velvet. I walked till my knees hit the bed. We fell together and rolled in the tousled sheets.

"Darling," she whispered, "don't be clumsy, darling. Don't be eager ..."

The velvet skin sought my hands, the full lips darted, bit. Thunder rolled in the night sky. It began to rain.

"In the rain, Johnny. Nicer. And it could be like this always. On the sand … Acapulco, France. Anywhere … so much, Johnny." Lips burned me between words. The thunder rolled and a flash of lightning lit the whole room but we were blind.

My name chattered in jerky rhythm in my ear. West Anniversary Drive snapped like a ribbon in the wind and threw the little stucco house high, high. We rode the turbulence of a summer storm, Edna and I, dark and wild; up and then swooping, looking down on the world and the warm rain fell and fell.

Friday was hung over. Friday was a cold egg and miserable, irritable downtown and working. Friday was Edna nervous and snappish, tender and loving, by turns. And the time flew. Friday was shorter than a creditor's greeting.

Worst of all—Friday was the day before Saturday. Saturdays I worked a half-day. Or I guess had worked is what I mean. First thing this Saturday morning I called the office. John Bellotte, the sales manager, was my immediate superior, and I talked to him. He knew about our cabin at Crestline. So I told him I was going to the mountains over the week-end and wanted an early start.

"Well, sure, Johnny, take the day." His booming salesman's voice rattled the diaphragm. I held it away from my ear. "Is that dish of yours going along? I mean the legal one, John boy."

He roared in appreciation. I waited until he ran down, then said, "That's the reason I'm going. Edna and I—Well, we had a thing, you know?"

"Oh, you don't have to explain to me, Johnny. I know how it is, my boy. Just go right ahead." His tone lowered. "I talked with Charley Dawson yesterday. John, my boy, I didn't know you had it in you. Magnificent."

Until that moment I hadn't thought of the possibility of Dawson spreading the story of the scene in the bar. But he had, evidently. For an instant I panicked, the hard purpose of the Plan dulled. Then I realized that it could only help. Sure. Johnny Babcock had a fight with his old lady. You hear about the thing in the York Club? Dawson says Babcock took this broad...

It would help. When they found my body.

"Johnny? Are you still there."

"Still here, John," I said into the phone. "I won't be in, then. Right?"

"Perfectly, perfectly."

"And do me a favor, John..."

"Yes? Just name it, boy. I'm in your corner."

"Don't say anything about the fight—me and Edna."

"Surely not. Surely not, Johnny."

"I mean, it's not another woman, really. I just want to drive to the place over Saturday, get boiled by myself. You know, for the good of my soul."

"They do say absence makes the heart, and so forth. You go ahead, Johnny."

"I'll be in Monday, so hold my check for me, huh?"

I thought that was a nice touch. Edna should be out of bed, seeing how I handled this. But she wasn't out of bed; she was sleeping, tousled and warm, all honey and spring steel. The thought squirmed in me.

John Bellotte said he would hold my check and hung up. I went to the kitchen and drank the coffee I'd poured before calling. It was cold. My eyes kept moving to a calendar on the wall. The top leaf said Friday. But that didn't fool me—this was the day that would change my life.

Edna was still in bed. I stood, dressed and ready to go, looking down at her sleeping form. One hand was draped over the edge of the low bed to the floor. I picked it up, tucked it under the silk sheet. She stirred, smiled in sleep, murmured. I kissed her quickly and the hot, sweet, woman-smell stayed with me all the way out to the car.

There were no thoughts in my mind. When our plan had solidified I became a man with a false purpose, dedicated to a proposition I was conditioned by my whole life to abhor. But I drove to town and I did what had to be done to get away with murder.

The freeway was line after honking, speeding line—as usual. Red morning sun hung high to the east and the air was heavy. This would be a scorcher, without smog. San Bernardino would be sweltering. I tooled the big convertible between cars without thinking about it, my motions automatic.

I was driving the new car because it was part of the plan. The Ford was at home again, in the garage. A Gardena bartender who knew me had sent it back yesterday. The Cadillac convertible was Edna's pride. This was the measure of her devotion to the plan— the car would be demolished. It was long and heavy, chromed and trimmed, a metallic pink hearse—which we couldn't afford and never should have bought.

No matter. Today the payments stopped.

In town, I picked a gas station at random. One of the big ones, loaded with cars. I'd brought along a five-gallon can. The attendant filled it with white gas, then gassed and checked the Cadillac.

"Six-eighty, mister," he said, wiping a spot of grease off the gleaming hood. "Nice car."

I nodded, paid him and left, tires protesting as I whipped out of the lot. At a super market on Figueroa I bought three pints of cheap wine. The liquor counter was crowded. I saw no one I knew. And it wouldn't have made any difference if I had.

Back downtown, I found a parking space on Hill and walked to Barney's liquor store. This was where we regularly dealt. Barney knew both Edna and me—he and I had gone to school together—and most of our crowd The store was small and very colorfully decorated with foil and chrome, smelling strangely of fresh-cut cardboard.

"Hi, Johnny," Barney greeted me as I stepped in from the street. He bustled up behind the long counter. "No work today, huh? What a racket."

I grunted, fumbled in my jacket pocket for a cigarette.

"What's the matter, kid? Start the week end early?"

"Barney, just get me a Walker red and shut up, will you?"

"Ah. Like that, is it?" He smiled knowingly. His hair was receding and his frowns ended where the hair had been, but smiles seemed to go all the way back. A nice guy, Barney. "So I'll get the red. I'm watching the store."

I picked up a rack of mix from a display and put it on the counter. Barney came back with the Scotch. There was no one else in the place. He looked toward the window, then winked at me.

"Want a touch?"

I grunted again, leaning a hip against the counter in what I hoped was an attitude of dejection. The cigarette smoke burned my eyes.

Barney snaked an open bottle from a hiding place, poured a quick dollop into two paper cups, hidden from passing eyes by a counter display. His eyes flicked to the window, back to me. He could lose his license for selling by the drink. But then he wasn't selling. He thought I needed a drink. A very nice little guy, Barney. I'd miss him. I'd miss a lot of things.

I cursed and snatched the paper cup, spilling the fiery stuff down in one swallow. Barney's eyes, bright and ferret-like, followed the action. His tongue clucked against the roof of his mouth.

"Edna?" he asked softly.

I looked at him, jaw stuck out. "Mind your own business, Barney." I wiped my mouth, picked up the stuff. "Put it on my tab, will you?"

"All right, Johnny." He sipped his own drink. "Don't let it get you, kid. Whatever it is, it ain't the end of the world."

"Okay, Barney. Okay."

"You going somewhere?"

"Mountains. Got to think, get stinking. Work it out."

"Sure." He touched my arm once, lightly. "Sure. See you next week. Little golf, maybe—Tuesday or Wednesday?"

I wanted to tell him then that there'd be no more golf for us; no more anything. I didn't. I just ran. The crowds pushed at me and I pushed back and the Scotch, sitting on cold coffee, began to growl. The warmth spread and by the time I reached the car I could break the seal on my own bottle without thinking at all.

I sat slumped on the hot leather, sipping from the bottle. I sat that way a long time. John Bellotte would tell everyone at the office that Edna and I had had a big fight. Stories like that never lose anything in the telling. Then Barney would noise his story around and there you had it. I was ready.

I glanced at my watch. One o'clock. No sense at all in putting it off any longer. I took a final suck at the bottle, corked it and dropped it on the floor between my feet. It was time. I knew, with a weird sort of disassociated clarity, that the moment I got the bum into the car I would be committed beyond recall.

A hundred thousand dollars' worth of life, darling! The sand—Spain, France. Us, Johnny—you and me...

The motor roared under my thrusting toe and I drove to the park like I expected it to leave before I got there. The same figures pressed the same grass; wilted palms waved dusty leaves at the idlers on the walks. I drove completely around it. I didn't see him. He wasn't there.

I stopped at the corner by the stone lions, tying up traffic. My horn blasted; was answered immediately by five or six behind me. I ignored them. He wasn't there, that's all there was to it. For an instant I was sure he wouldn't show. I saw the whole thing: I'd go home, tell Edna the man hadn't shown up and what could I do? She'd be very forgiving and loving and we could go on planning, half-serious, calling wonderful images of what we could do if we had a lot of money. And never, never, never—would we mention murder.

I saw him then. Waving over the heads of hurrying pedestrians, threading casually toward the car. Tall and skinny, but broad-shouldered—like a pro end. But he looked cleaner than last time. He'd shaved. That was all. He was the same man I had chosen to die for me.

"Hi," he said, climbing into the car. He slammed the door and the cars behind honked impatiently. "Told you, didn't I? One o'clock. Here I am."

He grinned. Brown teeth and red, red gums. The wine smell came to me, sour and fruity. He had drunk his breakfast. The horns objected behind. I turned the wheel, made the light and headed for the freeway.

"Say," he said, when we were moving swiftly through the Saturday traffic. "What's your name, anyhow? You never did tell me, did you?"

"Babcock," I said. What was the difference? "John Babcock. Call me Johnny."

He laughed at nothing and relaxed. One hand rubbed voluptuously over the smooth, red leather of the seat. I passed him a cigarette, lit one for myself.

"Nice car."

"Yeah. How about you?"

"Me? What do you mean?"

"Your name—what is it?"

"Oh. George Carter. I didn't tell you, huh?"

"You hadn't, no."

"Yep," he said, nodding several times as if to convince me beyond all doubt. "That's me, all right. Say, uh—Johnny. You ain't forgot about the heavy work?"

I looked at him, shook my head.

He muttered about his back and settled deeper in the seat. I threw my cigarette into the rushing air and concentrated on getting out of town. On the Santa Ana Freeway we picked up speed, one of a thousand rushing machines, all with secret destinations.

George Carter tried to say something but the wind snatched the words away. I shook my head at him, switched on the radio and turned it up loud. The wine I'd bought lay on the floor in a paper sack. I nudged the sack over to him with my left foot and indicated that he should open it. He did. When he saw the bottles he almost licked my hand.

Carter finished one pint without breathing. Then he began sucking slowly, with obvious enjoyment, on the second. By the time we had gotten through Pomona, roaring slightly upward toward Bernardino, he'd killed the second pint and passed out quietly on the seat, moving with the car's motion. I kicked around on the floor, got the Scotch up in my lap and the cork out. The drink almost wrapped me around a diesel tar rig. But I needed it. I corked the bottle, waved at the driver of the big, square tar-hauler, and settled down grimly to drive.

CHAPTER FIVE

The sun was high in a sky so clear that the only relief was thin tracings of jet vapor. When we got to San Bernardino I slowed for the city traffic and cursed silently and hotly while a burn of backed-up whisky gas rose in my chest.

The sun poured down. The throb in my temples had become a solid, pumping thing. I pulled off the main drag, rolled the Cad to a stop. My head fell back against the seat and my eyes closed. For a long while I sat like that.

Without the car's motion, the sun was just too much. I roused finally, started the engine and ran up the top, fastened it. Carter still slept. His third bottle was tightly clutched in one hand. I belched and got out of the car.

It was several blocks before I could find a place busy enough so that I wouldn't be particularly conspicuous just because I was a stranger. The one I finally chose was a bar. A hillbilly bar. I knew that because it was filled with jukey music from a sort of Taj Mahal with bubbles and sunlight from an enormous skylight. A happy place. Big and crowded. Even at four in the afternoon.

A long bar, running along one side, was loaded with stand-ees. Twenty or so round tables, all crowded with drinkers, spattered the rest of the large room. A laughing, shirt-sleeved bunch, shouting loudly over the blaring juke and drinking beer from the necks of bottles. I pushed in, stood for a moment at one side of the door, looking around. It suited my purpose fine.

"Hello, big fella." A tiny blonde girl stood in front of me. She was cute and young, a round tray clutched under one bare arm. "You drinking or looking?"

She wore an abbreviated costume of white halter and matching shorts and a wisp of green apron around her tanned middle. Her nice legs were bare and she wore white shoes held on with thongs tied around slim ankles. I couldn't help grinning at her. That's the kind of a girl she was.

"Could you bring me a real cold beer to the phone booth?"

"Sure, honey." She sidestepped a romping boy in a checked shirt, pushed him into the crowd at the bar with a robust shove. "What kind'd you like?"

A table clamored for her attention. She waved without turning and waited for my choice. I took her elbow, started threading through the crush toward the back of the place. It was dimmer there. And I saw the outline of a public phone.

"You kidnappin' me, mister?"

"Just borrowing you for a while. Will they mind?"

She grinned up. "They might. Say, you're pretty rangy. Might not do 'em any good to mind."

We reached the comparatively free space in front of the phone booth. It was shadowed, stacks of beer cases making a small cul-de-sac in the roaring joint. The girl blew a strand of silky, corn-colored hair out of her eyes and looked up at me, serious, questioning. Her lipstick had smeared at one corner and the smudge gave her mouth a perpetually curved effect. Very cute.

"You ain't from 'round here," she announced.

"Oh? How do you know?"

"You said borrow, just now. Folks 'round here say borry. Most of 'em. And it's awful hot for a jacket like that there. And a tie, yet. My goodness."

I looked down at the jacket. It was a lightweight nylon I'd donned that morning. It was drenched now at arm-pits, neck, and in back.

"Never thought about it," I said. "Get me that beer, five dollars' worth of quarters and buy yourself a mink ranch with the rest." I stuffed a ten-dollar note into the top of her apron. Her skin was soft and dry in spite of the heat. Where my fingers touched, anyway.

"I don't need 'em," she said.

"Mink ranch?"

"Oh." Her eyes crinkled at the corners. "I thought you said pink pants."

She took off for the bar, looking back over one tanned shoulder. I grinned after her for a moment, enjoying her walk. And the place. People work hard all week, save their money and energy while the living is earned and the bills are paid. With Saturday come a few beers, a little shuffleboard, scads of tear-jerky music and a healthy and humorous regard for the difference in the sexes—is that bad? And they have a ball, too. No cocktails and fancy clothes, no slinky women who value only their own beauty and ultra-slick conversation. Just beer and scrubbed faces and honest laughter. The equipment is the same all over. Sometimes it's disguised a little better.

I sighed and ducked into the phone booth. For a moment I'd forgotten my reason for being in the place. It all came back when the long distance connection was made. Including the lump in the stomach.

I waited for the Los Angeles operator to ring my home, drumming sweating fingers on the metal table. The booth was impossibly hot. I set the receiver down, dumped what change I had onto the ledge, and struggled out of my jacket. The folding door opened.

"Take the tie off, too," the waitress said. She stuck a cold, cold bottle of beer into my hand. "There. I got it myself. Coldest in the case."

"Thanks, honey. That's all. Shut the door."

I could hear the LA operator talking with Edna, explaining the call.

The girl didn't move. I glanced at her, motioned for the door to be closed. The cute face had stiffened, the smile warping—a wax smile, beginning to melt and then caught in the act. She reminded me of Dee in that moment. Dee, the little barfly I'd passed in the night. The same instant defensiveness—and a lurking sensitivity. The way she'd looked on the street just before we parted.

"The door, doll," I said, harsh with the knowledge that Edna would be on the wire in seconds. "Close it."

The smile dropped all the way off. She looked at me for a moment, her young face blank. Then she lifted her clenched hand and dribbled quarters all over my head. They bounced and slid, rattling off the phone, the table. She said nothing. Just walked away, hips swinging more than was necessary. She looked back once, tossed her head.

The operator asked for money and I snatched enough to satisfy her. The gong rang in the tight confines of the booth, accentuating the same sound in my head. When Edna's voice crackled out of the black instrument, I was ready to bite chunks out of the mouthpiece.

"Hello? This is the—"

"I know who it is."

"Johnny!" Her breath sucked in sharply. "What are you—"

"Shut up and listen a minute."

I took a quick gulp of cold beer; I felt it all the way down. Nothing had ever tasted that good. I gripped the phone.

"Things are a little different than we figured. Couple of items we didn't take into consideration. It's a nice day. The roads are loaded with cars. All kinds of traffic. Most of the highways will be choked till midnight and beyond by people coming home from Crestline and Lake Gregory."

"Well, what's that got to do with it?"

"Will you listen, I'll tell you. You can't drive up like we planned. Too much chance of seeing one of our week-ending neighbors. If they see me on the way up, it's all right. I'm supposed to be going to the cabin. But you're not. Nobody must see you."

"But how about—him, Johnny? Won't someone see him and wonder?"

"He's got a name." It came out colder than I intended. "I mean his name is Carter. George Carter. And he's asleep, all slumped down. Nobody'll see him, I'll see to that. Anyway, I won't go through Crestline till after dark. Or dusk."

"What do you want me to do, Johnny?"

"That's better." Boy, it was hot in that booth. I opened the door a crack; raucous sound crept in.

"Johnny, are you still there? Johnny..."

"I'm here, I'm here. It's hot in this booth." I tried to light a cigarette but my matches were wet, soaked with sweat. I cursed without caring. "Look," I said into the impersonal mouthpiece. "We have to play it by ear. Just enough to be safe. Here's the bit. You come in from the desert side. The desert side, got it?"

"Desert side. All right."

"When you get to Cedar Pines you'll be on the Crest Forest Road. You can't miss it."

"I know the Crest road," she said. "Go ahead."

"All right. Now, when you get to Seely Way, you turn north. Seely Way is the road we use to get up to our road. Except we come in from the other end, off the Seely Flat Road."

"I know, I know. And that way there's not much chance of running into any Crestline or San Moritz friends. That it?"

"That's it. I'll take care of—of my part. But if you're not where you're supposed to be..."

I pressed my face against the wet shoulder of my shirt. Edna breathed heavily in my ear.

"Johnny, I'll be there. I'll never let you down."

"Sure, sure," I said. "Look, I want you to leave right away, this minute."

"Right now? But why? It's hours till dark."

"Now, damn it. You can't make any kind of time in the Ford and I don't want you driving fast. A speed ticket would end it all."

The tinny voice cut in, requested more money. I got some quarters from the floor, cursing the waitress, and poked the coins into the slot. The gong rang again.

"Johnny?"

"I'm here. Now don't worry about this call. It's natural enough even if it becomes known. I laid a trail in town a mile wide. The story is you and I had a fight. By the time they find his—my body, it'll be well circulated."

"I hate that. People thinking I drove you to—" She stopped abruptly, whispered, "I'm sorry, darling. You go ahead. Remember I love you. And Johnny..."

"Yes, what is it? This booth is hot."

"Don't drink too much, will you? Please?"

"Edna, listen. Without something to drink, I'd never get through this mess."

"Be careful, darling. Be very careful."

"All right, all right. Listen to me, now. Park in the quarry cut-off, like I showed you. Don't, under any circumstances, come to the cabin. I'll take care of that."

"Yes, Johnny. But I'll be worrying—"

"Okay. So, worry. But stay in the car. The quarry road's been abandoned for years. It might be a little rough. It's only fifty yards or so from our place, east down the mountain. Park by the tool shed. Don't get out of the car. And don't throw anything out of it. Just sit."

"Sit and wait," she said, barely audible. "I will. But hurry, Johnny. I'll be terrified until you come."

I tried to take a drink of the beer while she spoke. The bottle rattled against my teeth. I set it on the floor, wiped sweat out of my eyes.

"I'll get there awful damn fast. You be ready."

"I wish—Johnny, you know what I wish?"

I sighed. "What do you wish, baby? It's too late to do a damn thing but what we're doing. And this one I don't aim to fumble. Now, what was it?"

She remained silent, thinking. I glanced out into the tavern. My little waitress was bent over the shuffleboard table, intent on pushing a weight to the far end. Around her, men jostled good-naturedly to get a clear view of her brown legs and well-filled shorts in that position. All were laughing. Beer bottles glinted in the sun slants from the skylight. The girl wiggled the portion under scrutiny, directed a remark over her shoulder and one man doubled over with mirth. The others hooted.

"Johnny?" Edna's voice came to me from the receiver. "You still there?"

I tore my eyes away from the scene and cleared my throat. Meanwhile, back at the murder ...

"Yes," I said. "Any questions?"

"No. I'll be there."

"Edna ... have you ever played shuffleboard?"

"Have I—Johnny, are you all right?"

"Look, all I asked was—Never mind. See you at the quarry. And I hope the money is worth it. I sure do."

"There's more to it than that, Johnny. Much more. Don't weaken now. Do one thing in your life all the way."

"Yeah, yeah." I kicked the bottle on the floor, spilled the beer. "What would you say if I called it off?"

There was silence. A deep and meaningful silence. I gripped the phone till my knuckles hurt. Then she said, "I don't think I could stand another defeat for you, darling."

The line hummed, seemingly very loud. I covered with my free hand, leaned against the pebbled-metal side of the booth. My breathing was ragged, burning my lips as it hissed into the mouthpiece. Finally Edna broke the silence.

"I'll be at the quarry road."

"All right."

"Don't think too much, darling. Just do what you have to, Johnny. All right?" She waited, breathing heavily. When I remained silent, she said, "I love you, Johnny. Don't ever forget that."

"Oh, for Christ's sake, Edna. Let's—"

A tinny click on the line announced the operator cutting in. I pronged the receiver and slumped in the seat. And just sat there. The walls of the booth inclined crazily.

"Who were you talkin' to?"

It was the waitress. She had nudged the door open and stood leaning against the side of the booth. A fine film of perspiration dotted her smooth face. The lipstick smudge was still there.

I shook my head at her and got out of the booth.

"You left your money."

I reached in, got the change off the shelf. The quarters on the floor would have to stay there. The juke erupted into a tune even louder than the one before. If that were possible. Anyway, it gave me an excuse not to talk to her. I didn't want to.

"Don't you like me, big fella?" Her hand caught my arm and held, fingers digging. I looked down. She was very young, very healthy, very serious.

"Sure I do," I said. "You're a doll. And I guess you know it. But—" I searched for a way to go on. There was none. I shrugged.

She dropped her eyes. "I didn't mean to bother you. I just thought—I mean, you looked so big and nice and sort of desperate standing there in the doorway. I usually don't make a fool of myself over men."

I lifted her chin with a finger. Her nice eyes were hurt and wet and a little bewildered. "Then, you're very lucky." I said softly. "Very lucky. Some people just naturally make fools of themselves. And know it all the time. It seems to be the way this funny old life is."

She smiled, slow and not very deep. She took a breath.

"Okay. So you're married."

I laughed. She took my arm and walked me to the door. There, I sobered. It was an odd feeling. Not that I wanted to make anything with this girl. But I might have. And the fact that I couldn't give her my name, maybe get her phone number, burned me. I saw just how final was this step I was to take. The girl ran both hands up my arm, gripped lightly.

"One drink? A quickie?"

I shook my head. "Good-by. And don't forget the pink pants. They might come in handy."

"Around here?" She shook her head, blinked and watched as I walked away. The jukey music poured into the bright sunlight. following me down the steaming pavement as I walked away.

I'd sweated through my clothes in the confinement of the phone booth and I was cold sober. All the Scotch I'd consumed had done nothing but leave a bad sort of taste in my mouth. And right then I had a funny feeling—a strange hunch that from now on I'd have trouble drinking enough to get drunk.

The price of a sawdust soul.

So I stopped at a liquor store and bought another fifth.

The Crest Highway was full of traffic as we began the long ascent. It was a good thing I'd told Edna to come in from the other side. Carter slept without movement. He was double drunk, the way only a wino can get drunk—utterly oblivious. The third bottle of wine had been tapped. It lay on the red leather, sloshing. About half empty already.

It was seven-thirty. Four hours to go. An orange sun squatted low over the ocean far away to the west while approaching night staked shadow claims on the eastern slopes. I found the old road I'd marked out for the wait—I didn't want to pass through the city of Crestline in daylight—and drove out of sight along its cracked and pitted asphalt length.

Night came on snail feet and it was somber when it arrived. The moon was a pale blur through heavy overcast and there was only an occasional glimpse of a star. I had the radio and my flitting thoughts for company. I preferred the radio.

And the bottle. That's what saved me. I sucked and sucked at it, chasing the burning stuff with the six-pack of mix I'd bought at Barney's. Every once in a while my eyes would wander to the sleeping form of George Carter. Sleep well, George. Dream. And leave the nightmares to me.

CHAPTER SIX

The cabin was a sweetheart. On the very summit of Viewpoint Knoll, it faced a deep canyon; the view from the porch was magnificent. The front yard sloped steeply for fifty yards and then dropped away to nothing. In the light of day the purple mountains in the distance almost assaulted the senses with their solemn magnitude.

Quiet. Wind-blown mountain quiet. Edna said it reminded her of the Ozark shack she'd spent her life trying to forget. In which cause two more lives were about to be squandered—mine and George Carter's.

I'd miss the cabin. It had been the family's week-end retreat for more years than I could recall. It was dark when we got there. Deep dark, like a root cellar at midnight. The wind had come up, singing over the rocks and through the sparse timber. It sounded a little like a dirge.

The cabin was dark and shuttered. I rolled the car past it and continued down the steep slope for fifty yards or so.

On the seat beside me, George Carter slept, twisting and mumbling once in a while. I reached over and shook him.

"Carter. Carter, wake up."

He didn't move. I started the engine, pushed the button to lower the top, and got ready to do what had to be done. Before I got out of the car I got the half-empty Scotch bottle and drank throat-searingly. My tongue was raw, my head hummed, and the hard lump under the ribs was back to stay. When I did get out, the ground wavered under my feet. There was no feeling of drunkenness, but my muscles answered reluctantly, my knees operated stiffly and seemingly independent of my wishes.

The first Scotch bottle—the one I'd bought at Barney's—I dropped by the parking space. Clue, you see. Yeah, man. Really swacked, old Johnny was. Had a fight with his old lady. You know Edna? Beautiful broad, man, but—What happened was he got loaded and forgot to push that brake all the way back. You know?

I went back to the car. Two empty wine bottles lay on the floor of the front seat somewhere. I had to get them. They would mess up the picture if they didn't melt. Moving very carefully— by this time it was difficult to make my mind give the necessary commands—I crawled into the car from the driver's side. The car was canted sharply with the frightening pitch of the slope. I felt around under Carter's sprawled legs. The bottles hid from me. I slid off the seat and lay on the ridged floormat, cursing without heat. It felt good like that. My face pressed the rubber. Smelled like tires—and airplane dope.

I sighed. Couldn't just lie there. Had to kill a man. I giggled at that. Me, kill a man. My outstretched hand brushed glass. A bottle. I reached. Carter snorted and turned and his hairy leg struck my hand. I reared, pulling back and whanging my head on the underside of the dash. Stars broke and pinwheeled. I cursed again and backed out of the car, and Edna almost collected the insurance for real.

The car had a safety parking brake on the left side, near the door. It was the foot type, like a clutch pedal, only hanging from above. The release was a small, knobbed lever on the dash cowling at the extreme left. I hit that with my shoulder, backing out. It was almost the last thing I ever did in this stinking life.

The ratchet on the brake chattered. Ground swept away from my hanging feet and the heavy car nosed down the pitch of the yard toward the lip of the canyon. The lurch threw me against the front of the seat, wedged me; the door closed on my dangling legs. The car bounded and slewed and heart jammed solidly into my windpipe. I couldn't make a sound.

I struggled to get out. My elbow hit the hanging brake pedal. I leaned on it in desperation. The steel bit my skin but I hardly felt it. Brake bands squealed, fighting against the weight of the Cadillac and the pull of the steep slope. The car slowed. My right hand found the foot brake and in that awkward position I brought the car to a sliding stop fifteen feet from the edge of a sheer drop of over two hundred feet. Breath roared into my mouth and I couldn't believe we hadn't gone over the lip. The whisky heaved in me.

The car was angled so steeply I was afraid to move, afraid I'd start the thing moving again. Carter had slid from the seat during the wild ride, now huddled on the floor. His eyes blinked, opened. He squirmed for a moment. Then his eyes closed again and he went back to the drugged sleep, head twisted under the heater. My heart started working again and my brain dripped like a ball of butter in the sun.

Carefully I removed my elbow from the emergency brake. The safety had caught. Then my right hand came away from the foot pedal. I rubbed my streaming face with the hand and felt ridges left in the flesh by the molded footrest.

I crawled out of the car, looked back at Carter. He lay as I'd left him. There was a black line against the red of the seat. I picked it up. A tire iron. I'd shoved it down behind the seat for later use. Now, I held it in two fingers, fighting to focus on it. Then the import of the heavy piece of steel got through to me. I dropped it on the seat, backed away.

I was sick behind the car. Roaring, hollering sick. Then I stumbled upward to the cabin. My legs were pipe cleaners; breath rasped in my throat. Sometime later, my feet hit the cabin steps, and I flopped forward on the cold boards of the porch and sobbed with relief.

I couldn't kill him. I never could have.

The ground was hard against my face. Frozen. Yes, the turf is frozen. In Long Beach? Don't be silly, Babcock. Get up, kid … get up, now. Johnny, Johnny. That-a-boy … you took that end out like why don't you take Delia Robinson to the hop, Johnny? She's a nice girl, no, Johnny don't. I'm afraid, Johnny, don't. Here they come! Three o'clock high and Johnny got 'em good, good old Johnny. Uncle Sam don't want me, parade or no parade. People. Always people—shouting football, cheering. Snaky parades and people shouting, Johnny, Johnny. Oh Johnny, Oh Johnny, how you can—

"Johnny!"

The whirling stopped.

"Johnny! Get up out of there!"

It was wood under my cheek, wet now with my tears and cold with the wind off the mountains. Memory came, chilling.

"Get up, you bastard! Get up, get up …"

Each sense came separately from wherever horror had sent them. My eyes were open and not seeing; then the legs appeared. I licked my lips and tasted blood. They were Edna's legs. Little shoes—rhinestones on the heels. Twenty-nine dollars, marked down from …

I sat up. It was Edna, standing Amazonian above me. My head began shaking from side to side and the grin on my lips was loose and silly. The Scotch had a grip.

"I need a drink," a voice said.

Was that me? Painfully I hawked and spat—molten lead scraped up from my throat and the passage opened. "Drink," I said again, more clearly this time.

"You need a backbone," Edna's voice said.

She gripped my hair, bent my head over her knee. "Look at you." Her eyes smoldered high above me like St. Elmo's fire on a plane wing. "You call yourself a man!"

She flung me forward and I fell over the edge of the porch, down the three steep steps. The walk was cold flagstone. My head hit it hard. The Babcock anger twitched, rolled over. I sat up again. She stood on the porch, pouring invective on my buzzing head. Edna, Edna; where did you go? Who is this grating woman? My legs came under me when I told them to; I got up. She quieted, took a step toward me.

"Johnny…"

"No. Get back!" I straightened, strengthened. "Just keep your hands off me."

"Johnny, don't be silly. What happened to you? I waited and waited and almost broke my leg on that damn mountain. What happened?"

Edna wearing an old shooting jacket of mine, skirt whipping around slim legs, hair blowing unconfined. Her eyes were piercing, intent. I took a step back.

"No." She said it softly. "Don't think about going. Don't even think about anything but what we came for." She came down the steps. "Why did you get drunk? Tonight, of all times? Why is the car almost over the cliff—and him still alive? Why, Johnny?"

"You came by the car?"

"I came by way of the canyon trail. From the old road."

Something told me then. She stepped close and gripped my arm. Her eyes were wild.

"You can go back, now. You hear, hero? You can go back and finish the job. Mama's here…"

She laughed. High and shrill, like everyone in the world was an idiot but her and how stupid we all were not to see it. I wrenched away from the nightmare laughter, knowing it could not be real. She had cracked under too much failure. Spineless

Johnny had pushed her too far. Her voice trailed after me as I pounded down the slope, sliding, half-falling.

The car loomed as a darker shadow in the black night. The wind was really working, now; it whistled in my ears as I reached the edge of the drop-off.

Edna came behind me. I glanced back, saw her picking her way down the rough slope. What light there was glanced off the chrome of the steeply canted machine. I steadied myself on the smooth rear fender, went to the front.

The front door on the passenger side was open. George Carter lay half in and half out of the front seat, on the floor. His right hand gripped a handful of dirt. His head lolled over the rubber step, hair almost touching the ground.

He was very messily dead.

She must have hit him twenty times. The tire iron lay on the seat, smearing the red leather. She was behind me, then, breathing loudly.

"You see, darling," she said, reaching for breath. "You see? It's all over. Now we live, Johnny. You and I."

I turned. Something in my eyes warned her.

"Don't, Johnny."

I said nothing. We stared at each other for a long time. Then she spoke, low and quiet.

"You're dead, Johnny. Face it. You set it up, you brought him up here." Her lips broke away from the perfect teeth in what was supposed to be a smile. "There's no way out, and there's not much time." She touched me on the chest. "Take off your clothes. Change with him. We're going ahead on schedule."

"Edna, this is wrong."

"It's done," she said, biting off the words. She shook hair out of her face. "Now we gather the profit. Change. Remember, the gas chamber's waiting."

Have you ever undressed a dead man? The body is loose and formless; cloth clings to the cooling flesh. It's grisly. I was sick twice getting Carter's clothes off of him and onto me. The darkness and the wind, Edna's calm exhortations—and the clammy feel of a dead man's shirt, flecked with blood.

"You're doing fine, darling. Take off your watch. Put it on his wrist."

I did. She moved up beside me at the open car door.

"He looks fine," she said and turned to me. In the faint light of the moon her face was clearly carved. Beautiful. So damned beautiful. "Johnny, it's almost done. It was for us, Johnny—both of us. Never doubt it."

Her tone was warm and the night was cold. I slid my hands under her jacket, along her firm sides. She came to me. I bent toward her lips and they opened for me. My head cleared, the muddled, lost feeling fled.

"Darling, hurry," she said, when the kiss was done. The front of the jacket rose and fell with her breathing. Her eyes were little mad fires.

I leaned over Carter, got the flashlight from the glove box. The car floor was a mess. Thick blood, looking strangely like colorless oil in the flash's puddle, lay in strings on the rubber. My bottle of Scotch had rolled to the driver's side. I reached across Carter, keeping my eyes from his head. I got the bottle. My fingers couldn't handle the cork. I smashed the neck against the door, poured my mouth full of the hot fluid.

"Me, too," Edna said and I handed it to her.

Then I moved the body to the driving side, wedged it there. The can of gas was in the trunk, tumbled against the back seat. I got it out and the cap off. I couldn't bring myself to pour gasoline over the body; the rest of the car got it, though. When it was soaked, engine to top-boot, I pried the locked gas cap off, threw the can over the side and lit a whole package of matches.

"Hurry, Johnny."

I flipped the matchbook. Flames leaped with a gasoline swoosh and lighted the rocky slope, throwing shadows.

"Can you find the Ford?" I shouted.

She nodded and spoke, the words lost in the roar of the fire. I pointed, told her to go. She did. The heat was intense near the car. I tried to reach in to flip the emergency brake lever. My fingers just touched it and the flame forced me back. I had to lean inward, over the body. The gasoline blazed. Any second it would reach the tank. The knob came under my fingers again and I pulled.

The Cadillac leaped forward, knocking me down. It ran to the edge like a rolling torch and dropped off into the gorge. I lay on the ground, a little stunned. Out of the corner of my eye I saw the fierce flame dull as the car dropped, then go out like a match in a high wind.

I heard a dull crash from deep in the canyon. I clawed to the brink and looked over. The car was a mass of blazing wreckage splashed far below. That was Johnny Babcock down there. I'd never really got to know him.

Now I was a man without a name, without a background. Either that or a murderer. There's a choice for you. Even though I hadn't struck the blow, I was as guilty. Accessory or perpetrator, it's all one.

Somebody dies and somebody pays.

It was wild country. There were no other cabins near ours downslope. It seemed to take hours to reach the quarry road as well as I knew the terrain. I stumbled over outcroppings and banged into stunted trees, racing headlong down the pitch-black slope.

Finally, I found the road. The shed. And the car.

Edna was waiting.

I wrenched open the door on the driver's side. Edna sat there, hands gripping the wheel. Her face was white in the utter gloom.

"I waited," she said.

"Move over."

"Darling, you see now that I need you, don't you? Don't you?" Her eyes grew enormous in the white face. "I waited."

"Move the hell over," I said and pushed at her.

She moved and I slid into the Ford, under the wheel. My whole body was taut and it took a while for the trembling to stop. Edna had enough sense not to talk. She sat huddled against the far door, watching me with a faint smile on her lips. Her hair had been combed and it hung over the collar of the jacket, swaying with her movements. Her legs were drawn up sideways on the seat, knees pointed at me; both hands lay palm up on rounded thighs. She waited.

"Well, there you are. Officially you're a widow."

She gave a little strangled cry and moved against me in one lithe spring, clutching my neck. Her hands forced my head back to the padded backrest and she knelt above me, looking down. Then she opened her lips and kissed me. I reached for her and my hand encountered bare flesh where her skirt had climbed. Edna moved against me and then we were tangled on the seat, holding tightly as if to ward off the world.

"I'm a rich widow, Johnny," she breathed against my lips. "And you're my man."

"Without a name," I said and she pulled away, flopping backwards.

She lay with her shoulders high on the opposite door, skirt awry, bosom heaving. Her eyes swept like spotlights over my face, stopped on my lips.

"You don't need a name. You have me."

She thrust away from the door with a twist of her shoulders. Her hands pushed aside the tweed jacket, cupped a swelling breast in each. She held them out to me.

"Johnny," she whispered. "Johnny, darling." Her head tilted back and her nostrils pinched together. She said my name again and it was a wail in the closed car.

You couldn't call it love. It was too furious, too jerky and savage. A fight, it was, and both of us emerged shaken and exhausted, cramped and weary from twisting in the confined front seat.

A breeze drifted in through the windwing. It was ridiculous, but I could swear there was a taint to the air. like sweetened pork fat, frying. ...

CHAPTER SEVEN

"A rich widow, darling," Edna said, whispering over the faint music from the car radio. "Rich and beautiful and eager to please."

The wind had sharpened. The car was warm enough but occasionally a draft from the open windwing would wash over my face, chilling the sweat. Edna had her head on my lap, eyes closed. Her lips moved and she spun words of luxury and indolence. I said nothing. A vast ache had swelled inside me. Like an empty sound-stage late at night, when the make-believe has ended.

I reached up and started the motor; Edna looked up sharply. The dash light spread a soft shine on her still-flushed features. Her arms rose slowly, grabbed my neck. She pulled herself up, wriggling past the steering wheel. Her lips touched mine, then stopped. Faces inches away from the other, we looked in each other's eyes. Edna stiffened slightly and something went out of her face; a curtain seemed to drop far back in her eyes. We kissed quickly and dryly and she moved to the other side of the seat.

"All right," she said. "Let's haul it out of here."

I switched on the headlights and pulled away. The road was a mess. I dodged potholes and cracks as best I could while keeping up the speed. There was enough time to get to town but none to spare.

"Johnny..."

"Yes?"

Edna turned on the seat, drew up her legs, tucking the skirt around them. She did it unconsciously. Her legs were firm and well-rounded and sitting like that showed them off. I flicked a glance at her, then turned back to the business of keeping the Ford on the winding mountain.

"Johnny, what if someone called while we've been gone? Shouldn't I have an alibi, or something?"

"Don't worry about it."

"Don't worry about it? Well, that's nice. What do you think we're playing here—canasta?"

I fumbled in my coat, realized too late that the clothes I wore belonged to George Carter. My hand crept out of the pocket; I rubbed it on the mohair of the seat.

"Johnny, answer me," Edna said.

"Give me a cigarette."

She lit two. I inhaled gratefully and let the smoke out slowly through my nostrils. Maybe it would wipe out that smell. The Ford hummed along, for once acting nicely. We made the turn off the Viewpoint Knoll road, headed for home. The radio crackled some, far from the city stations. The scratch was good counterpoint for the rock 'n roll records the late-night DJ played.

"There's blood on your—on that coat." Edna said.

I looked at her. She still sat sideways, head turning now and then to peer out the back window.

"You hit him pretty hard. When you hit people with iron bars, they bleed."

"Do we have to talk about it, Johnny?"

"We don't have to talk about anything."

The road loomed empty ahead and the night rushed by.

"What's wrong, Johnny?"

"Wrong? Nothing…"

"Yes, there is. You're—I don't know what it is, but you're different, somehow."

"All of a sudden?"

"Yes," she said positively. "All of a sudden. What's wrong with you?" She waited and when I didn't answer said: "Honey, don't you understand? We're rich. We can do anything we want to—whatever we please. You should be happy, gay."

"There's a dead man back there. Splashed all over the canyon floor." I wound open the window, flipped my glowing cigarette into the rushing air. "I'm a freak, maybe, but I don't feel real gay." I looked at her. "I don't feel gay at all."

She lifted her chin, pretended an interest in the road behind. Her cigarette burned unheeded in the ashtray. Choking clouds of smoke tendrilled upward.

"This is a strange conversation," she said after a while. "Isn't it?"

I just grunted. The radio strengthened as we neared San Bernardino. Highway 18 had little traffic. I was grateful for that.

"Will there be anything left of him, Johnny?"

"Not much. There'd better not be."

"What do you mean?"

"My prints are on file. The army, remember? We talked this all out weeks ago."

"I know, but I wondered …"

"Edna, will you put that cigarette out before I choke."

She dug the thing out of the tray, squashed it.

"Don't holler," she said quietly. "This is no time to lose your nerve—"

"Again. Go ahead, say it. Again."

"I didn't say that, Johnny. Let's not talk. It'll be better that way. We're too full of this thing, too—too …"

"Guilty," I supplied.

Her eyes slitted. Then she nodded, slumped down in the seat. For a moment we didn't talk about it. But what else was there?

"How will they know? About the money, I mean."

"The car went like a bomb. They'll find my stuff. Some of it, anyhow. Rings, watch—something. Maybe not."

"Then how—"

"Look, you'll get the God-damned money! Who else would it be? Below our cabin, in our car? He's my general size. All my stuff is on him. You'll get the money. Now shut up about it."

"Shut up? What do you think we did it for, experience? Certainly, I'm worried about the money. What have we done, if we don't get it?"

"Yes, yes." I poured the Ford into a curve much too fast, slacked it down quickly on the other side. "They'll think it's me, you hear? I guarantee it. It's a guy named George Carter. A guy who wanted to earn an easy buck. But they'll think it's me. All your cares are past, Edna. Johnny Babcock is dead. And you'll get the money."

"I hate a sanctimonious bastard," Edna said. "Yes, you Johnny pure! Who the hell do you think you're kidding? You did it for the money, too. And don't deny it."

I slowed the Ford to a crawl. A diesel truck and trailer blasted, passed with a rush. I looked at Edna for a long, long moment. My wife. Until death do us part. In sickness and in health.

Whose death, Reverend—whose death does it have to be?

"Sure, Edna. That's what we did it for."

My fingers nudged the radio up to full volume. I glued my eyes to the road. If she said anything the rest of the way into Los Angeles I didn't hear it. The Freeway was clear of traffic. We raised LA about five o'clock in the morning.

Downtown cast a pale glow upward. Edna sulked in her corner, tilting her face to the night breeze, smoking incessantly. Whenever our glances met, she looked away. Just before we turned off the Freeway, she spoke, voice low and without any noticeable feeling.

"Back there, Johnny," she said, blowing smoke. "You might as well have swung that tire iron yourself, you know."

"Edna, let's not rehash. It's done. Forget it."

"No. This has to be said." She leaned forward, hugging her knees. "You negotiated for the policy. You spread stories of our fight. You bought the gas, bribed the bum."

"What are you trying to say?"

"I've said it." She turned to me. "You're it, kid. That's the only way it stacks if the cops ever get you. There's a dead man out in that canyon. Sure, I'm going to collect the money. Yes, I'm an accomplice. But your face fits the picture far better than mine—no matter who killed him."

"It matters to me." I slowed for a police car, my stomach tightened and I wondered if it would be like that from now on. "You, an accomplice. That's a big fat laugh."

"So laugh," she said, shrugging. "I'm telling you how it will look to the cops. If they have reason to look. And I'll hang you out to dry, darling, if you spill your yellow guts. Remember it."

The way she said it—so quiet, so reasonable.

The tires screamed as I bent the Ford around a turn. I fought the wheel. The speed had crept up with my agitation.

"Leave it alone, Edna. I know what we've done. I'm not ducking the responsibility. And I'm guilty of more than you think. But I don't want to talk about it."

She laughed. "Oh, Johnny, I love you. You kill me. Show your muscles, darling. It's a little late, but flex for Mama."

I bent over the wheel. It was hard to breathe. I had never really known this woman, and I didn't understand her now, when it mattered.

The streets downtown were glazed with that strange moisture of early morning, big city deadness which reflects streetlamp gleams and pale moon streaks sneaking between buildings. The long concrete corridors were empty. The city was as quiet as it ever gets; just the throaty overtone of a million shifting souls existing collectively. No activity. A cop, a cab, a late worker.

As I drove through the deserted streets. a strange feeling came to me. These were creatures of the night—shadow figures, drifting, sliding, never really seen. This was to be my lot. A card-carrying member of the same lodge. Welcome, Babcock.

What's in a name? Yeah. A rose by any other might smell as sweet—but it wouldn't be a rose.

I turned at the Bus station, followed the narrow street of closed shops and warehouse fronts for a short distance. Then I stopped the Ford in the middle of a block, pulling into the curb. My fingers clicked switches. The cooling engine creaked loudly in the sudden quiet, like an over-loaded winch cable.

Edna stirred. She sat up, made a face.

"Well..." she said.

It just hung there. I sat. From the moment the brake had slipped, my actions had been half-drugged, undictated by reason. A man was dead and the world would never be exactly the same again. I sat there and looked out upon the shapeless night.

"Johnny..."

"You better go home, Edna."

"No, Johnny, listen..."

"There's no time. Go home. If they find the wreck tonight and run a make on it, you could have early visitors." I pushed the door handle down. "Telling you that your loving husband had an accident."

"Tonight? You mean they'll come tonight? This morning?

"It could happen." I shifted on the seat and stretched cramped muscles. The ill-fitting suit tightened at shoulder and crotch. "Well, it's over, anyway. One way or the other."

I pushed the door open, got out. I rolled the window down and shut the door and stuck my head through the opening.

"Give me some money. It'll be three or four weeks before I can risk contacting you."

"You think they'll be suspicious?"

"You'll find out. Freese'll be tough. He didn't like the deal in the first place. He'll be real tough. You'll have insurance investigators for breakfast, dinner and supper for the next month. But play it easy…" The thread eluded me and I let it go. What was the use of pretense? I didn't care about the money. About Edna. About anything at all.

Edna handed me a bunch of bills. I stuffed them into my pocket without examination.

"They can't prove a thing, Johnny. Can they? Nothing at all. So let 'em bitch, let 'em prowl." She slid over under the wheel. There was a strange expression in her eyes. "I'll take care of the money part. Don't worry."

"Yeah, you will. You're a good actress. I can swear to that. Don't start fooling yourself, though."

I got my head out of the car, looked off down the street. There wasn't a thought in my head. Nothing. Only that Carter's coat wasn't thick enough.

"When will they pay? How long will it be?"

"The money?" I turned. "What?"

"Money, honey—coin of the realm. Wake up, Johnny. When will I get it?"

"About a month," I said. "Maybe less. Depends. But they'll pay. They won't like it, but they'll pay."

She licked her lower lip. "Cash, Johnny? Will it be in cash?"

"What? Oh, no, I don't think so. I don't know, Edna. My head hurts. Look, I'll call you when I can."

"Certified check?"

"Yes, I'd imagine. That's it." She expected more reaction. I worked up a stiff grin for her. "How's it feel?"

"How does what feel?"

"Well, I've never had a hundred thousand dollars before. I don't feel any better for it. But maybe that'll wear off."

Edna slipped the car into gear, rocked it gently with the accelerator. There was a tight, nasty smile curling her mouth.

"Johnny," she said flatly. "You haven't got a hundred thousand dollars. What I just gave you, that's all you get. You see, you're dead, baby. Very, very dead."

For a moment the silly grin stayed on my face, frozen there. Then what she'd said echoed and came back around.

"Wait a minute. You're joking. What—" I gripped the door, bowing to see her face in the interior gloom.

"'Let's not have a scene, Johnny," she said, leaning away. "The money's mine. All of it. Did you kill him? No! Because you didn't have the guts. Well, you're not cashing in on me. You're a slob and that's all you'll ever be."

"Wait, Edna. You don't know what you're saying. I love you! I was willing to kill for us. For you and me."

"Us!" She spat the word out. "Us, my eye. You poor slob. Do you think you're man enough for me?"

"Edna, don't call me that again."

"Slob! You are a slob. A gutless, suburban slob! Get your hands off that door!"

Her toe stabbed the accelerator, racing the engine; the car inched forward.

"No!" I said, and it came out a shout. "Edna..."

The door was locked from inside. I reached through the window, clutching at her. The motor roared and the car jumped forward; I scrambled alongside trying to get a grip on her. On that lying throat. Just one hand...

The car moved down the street. Slowly at first, then faster, dragging me. Edna bent away, raked a hand over my face, nails slicing my flesh. A burst of acceleration tore my fingers loose and flung me into the street.

The wet concrete was cool. I moved my face against it. There was an ache up there, a big one. The Ford's whine faded in the night. Then, above the noise of the engine, I thought I heard a peal of high, wild laughter. The laugh stayed after the car had gone. Long after, echoing in my head. Hollow goodbye to Johnny Babcock.

Johnny Babcock was a name on an insurance policy. A High School letter. Johnny Babcock was a smile drifting in a thousand places and a tipped hat wherever convention rode. An office collection, was Johnny Babcock, and a grieving widow.

No tears.

My mother cried when I got married. Tears enough for anybody.

CHAPTER EIGHT

The brotherhood is exclusive and demanding, but not snobbish. Members from all walks of life claim allegiance. The high and the low, the one-time rich and the one-time poor. And the rules are loose. Age is no factor and education has no bearing; abilities are nothing because the Brotherhood has no use for them. What the Brotherhood demands is your pride. All of it, payable on admission.

How prideful can you be four weeks without a bath and half as long without shaving? Too sober to lie down and too drunk to walk? Where is pride when the wine money doesn't come and the skinny, tough, abused, growling stomach whimpers for something besides its own juices to churn upon? A man, braced for a lousy nickel, looks down a nose red-veined from good living and says, "Go to work, you bum!"—where is it then?

Ah, but the days blend. They run together. One day it's Sunday and the Good Fellowship Mission spreads a fine meal in honor of Easter; and the next a newsboy hawks an edition, crying that the World Series is over for another year. Like level country from an airplane; a time exposure of a moving object, it's all one blur. No sun and no moon, no cold and no pain. Just a hazy in-between diffused by fruity alcohol and measured by the length of time between drinks.

No one asks your name or where you're from. No one cares. The wine sustains you. The blessed sugar—fine sifting euphoria during which no energy is necessary. Thirty-seven cents. Twice a day. The clouds roll in and the world is anything you want it to be.

That's the way it was. After Edna, I fitted right in.

JOHNNY, you got a puh—piece of match?"

"What for?"

"You got one?"

"No."

The air was cool. Moments ago the whistle on the aluminum company had sounded the lunch break. The day should have been warming up. But it wasn't. The street was dotted with men in all sorts of positions. Some lay in doorways, some squatted against buildings, some stood. A few. All were dirty and all were red-eyed and blearily hopeful in the new day's coming. It was noisy, too. But I didn't hear sounds anymore. After a while everything is drowned in the bubbling of blood in your own head.

"Johnny. Ask Montrose if he's got a muh—match?"

"What do you want with a match, Darby? You don't have anything to smoke. Do you?"

There was no answer. I rolled over in the doorway where I'd spent the night with my two friends. Darby Danbury squatted just outside on the sidewalk. His coveralls, dirty and patched, and his old plaid jacket contrasted to the whitewashed wall of the Mission. He dropped his head as I scooted out beside him. The light was strong. He looked at me, tried to speak. Nothing came out but sounds with no meaning and a steady spray of saliva.

Darby had been a fighter. A ruthless manager and little talent for pushing leather had combined to ruin his face, destroy his confidence and completely remove any courage he might have had. Now, he wouldn't fight a baby for a pint of wine. On Fifth street, that's saying something. When Darby was excited, or tried to talk too fast, his speech got tangled to the point of incoherence.

"You hear me, Darb?"

"Ah, now, Juh—Johnny. I guh—I—"

"Slow down." I sat up, rubbed my burning eyes. The concrete was cold and my pants were thin. "Where you been?"

Darby took a breath, turned a grimed and bearded face to me. His leather-visored cap hung over one ear. The absolutely flattened nostrils vibrated with air as he spoke.

"You and Montrose was sleeping," he said, enunciating slowly and carefully. "I got up. I—I went to the Paramount. Where my friend cleans. Yuh—you know?"

He pulled a big-knuckled hand out of the jacket pocket, opened it slowly. It was full of cigarette butts. Big ones.

"Is that—Is that good, Johnny? Ain't it, huh?"

"Darby, my son, quit your infernal sniveling."

Montrose stirred in the doorway, his deep tones sifting out into the pale sunlight. He struggled out beside me, propelling himself with pushes on the ground.

"Bad day," he announced. Hs eyes surveyed the haze with morning-squint.

I took a couple of the butts from Darby's hand, held one out to Montrose. who left off scratching his beard to take it. He fumbled up a match and we all lit morning smokes. Darby puffed furiously, lighting one of the ends after another, his battered face screwed up in concentration.

"I like the ones with liptis—luh—lisput—"

"Lipstick."

"Yeah." Darby grinned. "That. They taste better. Now I bet this here one—this one, see, I bet was a big, blonde, stallion girl, huh? With buh-bangs, maybe. And a tall, f-fine figure…"

"Shut up, Darby." I shouldered him aside and slumped beside him on the wall. My ragged felt crept down over my forehead. "Stop talking about it, Darby. I told you about it before."

"I'm sorry, Johnny. Y-you know I am, don't you, Juh-Johnny?"

"Darby, boy, don't worry about Johnny." Montrose grunted, shifted position on the concrete. "He's sour on women. You go ahead and like the lipstick. Ah, it is good. Here's some that's almost purple."

I glowered, said nothing. Darby made noises. Montrose rambled on.

"Johnny, my boy, you'd better take a long, cool look at your balance sheet. You should, indeed. No call to pick on Darby. Now, it's a bad day. In truth it is. But we're fortunate—the world is still here. I must admit that always surprises me when I consider some of the places I've chosen to rest my head. But there it is. A benevolent somebody or something will provide a sparkling short dog for breakfast. All, I promise you, will be serene."

"You shut up, too, old man." I coughed tried to loosen the wet sleep and sour wine in my throat. "What's the world here for? Who needs it?"

Montrose took a careful puff of a filter-tipped butt and stroked his straggling white whiskers, pressed and snarled where he'd lain in sleep.

"Johnny, boy," he said, "we need it. You and I. And Darby. God's chosen, we are. Who is more at ease, least eaten up with ulcers? Who has but to wake and the day is made? Who carries the bright beauty of a spoken—"

"I got ulcers. I got—" Darby's tongue tangled and he stopped. Montrose shook his head.

"You're an old fake," I said. "I don't want to hear your muscatel philosophy. Not this ugly morning."

The old man shrugged. His milky eyes swept the surrounding area. The members were waking. Here and there, out of doorways and ratty rooms, out of alley-ways and from under stacks of paper and cardboard, they came. New day. More wine.

Fifth is a business street. For about five blocks, just east of Main, it's only business is derelict. Liquor stores crowd used clothing emporiums; cheap, cheap restaurants separate cheaper bars. A few enterprising Nipponese groceries. Pawn shops, windows telling the story of poverty and day to day scrabbling. Automobile parking is allowed along Fifth street. But no one parks there. Park along a boulevard of broken lives where hubcap stealing is a profession? Don't be silly.

"Johnny," Darby said. He crept close and his stink offended me again. It always did. That, I hadn't gotten used to, even though I smelled as bad. "Johnny, l-listen … we guh—got to—" he sputtered off to nothing, spraying.

"Slow down," I said, automatically.

"Yeah. Look, I'm thirsty. What we gonna do today, huh, Johnny?"

Montrose heaved a great sigh. He took a gap-toothed comb from the front pocket of his greasy coat. He was going to curry his beard. It was a daily ritual. He would comb and scrape, separate and fondle each silken hair til the white mass gleamed. Then was he ready to meet the challenge of existence. Maybe that's what I needed. My own wouldn't do. It was black and thick, and evil-smelling and matted with dirt. Mine was a mask.

"Johnny, I'm thirsty. What we gonna do today, huh, Johnny?"

"You asked that," Montrose said. He pulled a piece of chewing gum out of his beard, cursing at the momentary pain.

"Anybody got any change at all?" I asked.

Montrose shook his head, busy with the beard. Darby said he hadn't any. And his eyes were clear so I knew he wasn't lying; there was no way Darby could lie and get away with it. His pale eyes slid like bubbles in a carpenter's level when he tried.

"Well," I said. "What'll it be, then?"

"Spark p-plugs, huh?"

I straightened and spat out into the street. A passing man cursed at me and I wiggled four fingers at him, thumb to nose. Working stiff. The concrete was cold and it wasn't getting any warmer. My body felt numb. Except for my stomach. There, the craving lived. And it came more awake with each passing moment. Darby was right about that. We had to get some juice. A short dog to wake up on.

"No spark plugs. I don't like that."

"I can't figure you, Johnny." Montrose stroked the feeble comb through his sidewhiskers. "You don't like to boost spark plugs. You won't let us steal hubcaps. Yet every time Darby asks you to go with him to work a day, you fly into one of your weird rages." The old man's shrewd eyes turned to me. "Would you rather stem? You're not very good at it, you know."

I had no answer for him. He turned his attention back to the beard. I had no answer for Darby, either. They had carried me for weeks, now. Oh, we braced the downtown streets together, stemming the fresh-faced workers as they hurried to lunch or for coffee. But I was no good at it. It takes a particular talent; either an absolute feeling of humbleness or a deep contempt, neither of which I could muster. One time I had begged a business man on Spring street for a dime. He had reached for his wallet and I had turned away without waiting for the money. The man had been a salesman for a rival steel firm. I'd known him once, very well. The experience made me wary of the streets for days. Only the insistence of the craving had driven me back.

While Edna tried to spend a hundred thousand dollars. No. That's what you're not to think about, Babcock. That's—

Edna. There it was, after all these weeks.

The name cut through the fog in my head and hung, plastered to the inside of my forehead where my eyes had turned. I cried out and slammed my hand down on the concrete. Darby jumped and began stuttering, trying clumsily to comfort me. I couldn't open my eyes. The lids squeezed of their own volition. I started.

"Johnny. Juh-Johnny, don't do that..."

Darby was shaking me. I opened my eyes and red flecks danced on my vision as the blood drained from my brain. I pulled my knees up to my chest and wrapped my arms around them. My head spun.

"You went away, Johnny. Y-you went away again."

My clasped hands trembled. Montrose leaned toward me, questioning with his wise, faded, old, mistrustful eyes. I grinned weakly.

"I'm all right. Need a wakeup."

We all settled back while the street activity quickened. Directly across from our doorway was a wine shop. The name liquor store would dignify it, but it wouldn't be true. Sam sold wine in bulk and in bottles and very little else. The shop, at the moment, was playing host to a steady stream of ragged men. They came out, clutching bottles, and walked quickly to the nearest alley or deep doorway. A brand new day. Some meet it one way, some another. On the street you learn to respect that difference.

"If we had a dime one of use could g-get a-a—"

"We haven't," Montrose said. "Johnny, it looks like the stem, son. And you'll never make it. Not today." He studies me for a long moment, whiskers twitching. "You better take a little better care of yourself. You haven't been with it long enough to just forget eating. Now Darby, he can go weeks. But you..."

"I'm fine, I told you." I turned a shoulder to the old man. Darby watched me anxiously. He was picking his nose, one big finger stuffed almost hurtingly into the shapeless blob of flesh the exploiters of the manly art had left for a nose. "Stop that! You'll hurt yourself."

"Well, g-gee, Johnny. I'm thirsty..."

I heard Montrose scuffling behind me. He got to his feet, wheezing. "Any ideas, Johnny?"

I shook my head, still full of the remembrance of my wife. Darby stood, stretched. His tough brown hair poked out around the leather-visored cap. He looked across the street, shook his shoulders.

"See," he said, shuffling a little, "Those guys got their juice. Looka there, Johnny. What we gonna do, Johnny?"

"Darby, I'm not your father," I said.

Montrose glanced at me sharply. I coughed, pulling the hat down to cover my mouth. Montrose lit another butt, handed one to me.

"Day work," he said. "You and Darby. I'm too old for that. I'll bum Maggie for carfare and work my route. We'll meet at the Doniker about five."

"No day work," I said. I flipped the butt.

Darby squatted in front of me. His big hand touched my knee lightly, went away.

"Y-you feel bad, Johnny? You take it easy. I'll work for us today. They's lots of things—"

I straightened, stretched my neck muscles. The trembling had spread to my lips. Pretty soon I had to have a drink. Darby's vague eyes rested on me.

"Stay there, Johnny. You—y-you stay right there."

"No. We'll stem. You and me, Darby." I turned to Montrose. "We'll be at the Doniker."

"Johnny, boy, wouldn't you rather work? Darby knows the men in the daywork section at the employment service. He could duke you in."

"If I wanted to work I wouldn't be on the grape, would I? Go ahead, hit your route."

The old man had a suburban route which periodically netted him a small change fortune. I didn't know what story he used but it must have been a good one. Pickings are always better away from the downtown section.

"All right," Montrose said, getting up. He was spry for a man seventy years old. "Johnny, didn't you once tell me you could play piano?"

I got up, stood unsteadily. Darby grabbed my arm. "Yes. Maybe I told you. It was a long time ago."

"Can you play well? I mean, in a bar, like? The old standards, so on?"

"One time, Montrose, I thought I was going to be a great pianist. Classics. concerts." I smiled, remembering. "The war came along. Instead of Juilliard I went to gunnery school."

"But you can still play?"

"Give me a butt, Darby." I leaned my back against the building. Lately it was hard for me to stand. I couldn't remember my last meal. I twisted, answered Montrose. "Yes, I can play. Any musician with a conservatory background can play honky-tonk piano."

"Johnny, we—we gonna stem?" Darby shuffled around.

"In a minute, Darb. Why, old man? What difference does it make?"

"Well, Maggie's got a piano. Bought it from the Good Will people. Oh, it's probably not in tune, I guess. But you could—"

"Maggie? You mean in the Doniker?"

"Yes." Montrose brushed aside his whiskers for a last suck at a short butt, threw the thing away. "Why not? Even drunks like music. Maybe especially drunks, depending on how you look at it. She'd pay you something. Not much, probably. Enough to drink on. Then

you wouldn't have to steal—which you won't do anyhow. Or stem—which you can't do."

"No."

"There it is again." The old man walked around in front of me. "Anything puts you in contact with people, you reject. You got to come out of that, boy. You're afraid to work, you can't beg and you don't want to steal. I'm a sonofabitch, son, I just don't see how you figure to make it."

"Johnny..."

"All right, Darb." I pushed away from the building, took a step. The legs worked. "You quit trying to figure me out, old man. See you at five."

But we didn't leave. Darby ran into Bottle Benny at the corner of the alley. He came back toward us, Darby did, leading Benny and stuttering like mad.

"Johnny," Montrose said, stroking his beard nervously, "I do believe he's trying to say Benny's willing to trust us."

"Yeah."

I looked eagerly at the shapeless coat the twisted little man wore. It was huge. Dirty and huge. Benny had been known to carry thirty bottles in his clothes without any visible lumps. His own frame must have been skeletal; you couldn't tell with the beard and the clothes.

"Hi, Johnny—Montrose. Darby here, he says you boys'd go for a short dog on the cuff." He cackled and scratched. "Might let one go for four bits."

Bottle Benny stood blinking in the unaccustomed light. Unaccustomed because he spent his life in alleys. Particular alleys. Those surrounding the area in Los Angeles known as Skid Row. Benny was a drainer. The drainer is a successful wino— that is, one who's made a routine that keeps him drinking and not working. Every day and night hundreds of bottles of cheap wine are bought and consumed. Mostly in alleys. Or doorways. When a man has approached or attained satiation, he occasionally throws his bottle away with a drop or two—or a dram or two—still remaining. The drainer exists on these dregs.

With two large empties suspended from a string around his neck, he patrols the alleys. What's left in all dropped bottles, he drains, with infinite patience and total disregard for brand or flavor, into his carrying bottles.

"Not four bits," I told Benny. "Two bits. You know we'll pay."

The wizened man cackled and shook his head. The wine had him goofy already. He'd had his wakeup. My stomach flipped and a dizzy spell gripped me. I leaned against the plate glass of a pawn shop. Pink spots blipped on my closed lids. When I was all right again, I saw Montrose and Darby walking Benny to the alley, arms across his bowed shoulders.

They came back with a muddy pint.

Darby pulled it from under his jacket, looked around quickly. Montrose snuffled and told him to hurry. I couldn't say anything. My throat had constricted; a spasm twisted my stomach.

"Puh—pretty li'l old short dog," Darby crooned. He lifted the pint, shook it. The liquor was a brownish red color with little bits of residue floating in it. "Benny hadda give us good stuff. We watched him pour it, Johnny. Huh, Montrose, huh?"

"Yes, son, yes. Are you drinking or not?"

He reached for the bottle and Darby jerked it back, his weak eyes darkening.

"No," he said, and his tone brooked no argument. "Johnny. Johnny first. He's sick."

"Well, then hurry up. My route takes three or four hours. Three good hours. Don't take it all, John! Darby, get it."

The warm, bitter liquid hit my stomach and spread like a woman's blush. I handed the bottle to Montrose and leaned against the glass and waited for the soothing heat to unknot cramped muscles. So good. Food. Fire. Dulling the knives.

When I opened my eyes, the old man had gone. I could see him shuffling away towards the Doniker, further down. Darby stood quietly, staring at me with his disconcerting directness. He blinked. The bottle was clutched in one dirty hand. The stubble of beard—Darby customarily shaved every day to avoid being arrested—made him look like a movie pug, made up for a punch drunk scene. Only Darby wasn't punchy from punches alone.

"What we gonna do, Johnny?"

"I don't know." I rubbed a hand over my forehead. It was clammy. "But we got to do something."

"Tuh—today's bad, huh, Johnny? I can tell." He held out the bottle. He hadn't yet had his wakeup. "Here. You t-take this too. I'll make it tuh-til we—"

"No." I straightened. You'd have to know how it is on Fifth to realize how much of a sacrifice that would be. A man's wakeup is sacred. "No, Darb. You drink it. Go ahead. I'm pampering myself. I feel fine. I'm all right. But today, Darb, we got to eat. I mean, really eat."

"You mean food?"

"Yes. Let's go."

The street didn't look so bad, now. The wine wiggled inside me, shooting out tendrils of heat. Pretty soon I'd be all right. Warm all over. Darby trotted beside me, wiping his mouth. His lips had tightened.

"Long's we're gonna eat. Johnny, we might as well restaurant, huh?"

"It's a little late."

"Yeah. But you d-don't like stemming. We can get enough in an hour to make a duh-dollar'r two."

I didn't care. Anything was better than bracing people on downtown streets. The same streets Johnny Babcock had walked so confidently just a few short weeks—or was it months?—before.

"All right. We can hit the hotels. Not the big ones. The ones on Main and Broadway, maybe."

"Suh-sure," Darby said, and grinned.

For him it was a good day. But for me it was a day I hadn't wanted to face. Suddenly, after months of merciful blankness, wine-fog and drifting shapes, I was thinking of a guy named Johnny Babcock. And a woman named Edna.

And a hundred thousand dollars.

CHAPTER NINE

Edna was doing just fine. She had moved out of the house on West Anniversary Drive soon after the insurance company settled the policy. They hadn't given up easily. For weeks the litigation dragged on. They took it to court, of course, undoubtedly influenced by Albert Freese. But finally there was nothing to do but assuage the grief of Mrs. John Babcock with the premium payment on a fifty thousand life policy—doubled because of the accidental nature of the holder's death.

That's the tack the company lawyers had used. They maintained that in the state of mind John Babcock exhibited on the day he died, a man would be more apt to deliberately drive over a cliff than to drink himself to death and then let his car roll off accidentally.

But Edna had prevailed. Pictures in local tabloids showed her wan and tragic, classic features molded in expressions of brave suffering. Still beautiful. She'd always be that.

I hadn't seen her in person. Hadn't tried. Day-old newspapers and an occasional radio report, heard at some shoeshine stand or other, were my sources. I didn't dare approach her. Even when the money she'd given me ran out—exhausted quickly in those first, frantic days on whiskey and self-pitying indulgences—I was afraid to contact her. She held all the cards. True. she would lose the money, perhaps go to jail, if it was discovered that John Babcock still lived. But I would go to the gas chamber. For sure.

I didn't want to die. Not like that; for a crime I hadn't committed. One, I knew now, I could never have committed. To protect myself, I had to protect her. That meant avoiding all the people I'd ever known, staying away from the thousand and one places a man learns in growing up. People passed on the street, glanced briefly at the tattered wino with the wild beard and hurt eyes, then looked away without interest. Some of them had known me well. There was a peculiar kind of pain in not being able to cry out after them.

Gradually I'd drifted into the limbo existence of the Skid Row Brotherhood. And for a blessed time, a curious sort of blankness enveloped me. I could not think of Johnny Babcock. Or Edna. Or George Carter. The thoughts just would not come. Once in a while a night visitation recalled the horror of the scene on the mountain. But not often. I blended more and more into the hollow-cheeked anonymity of Fifth street. I lost weight, added gray to my hair and beard and acquired even more picturesque stains for the filthy rags I wore.

And in my mind, deep in the oil-clicking file where memory lives, a block shut out all the remembrances of living and growing up; abnegating old ambitions, erasing dreams and blotting the past. Some sort of a tranquillizing syndrome, I guess. Maybe activated by the shock.

And the wine.

But today I'd begun to think again. Three times since waking in the cold doorway, I had seen Edna's name, and my own, in my usually placid thoughts. Darby and I walked the crowded streets while confusion seethed in me. I had no idea what we were doing or where we went.

"Johnny, I got a quarter from that chef. But—b-but nuh—"

"Slow it down, Darb. Take it easy."

The shifting downtown street, busy in the after-lunch rush period, came slowly to focus. I turned to Darby who stood beside me, shuffling and trying vainly to bring his lips under control.

"A qua-quarter, Johnny," he said finally, showing the coin in his palm. "But no food. Said the house had a rule."

"All right." I pressed against a building to let a fat, salesman-type past. "Look, Darb. We got to move pretty quick. It's almost one."

"Johnny, I got an idea. We—"

I took his hard-muscled arm, led him out of the stream of pedestrian traffic. I sneaked a look in the plate glass window we stood before. No wonder they stared. No wonder, at all. Be a wonder if they hadn't.

"Juh-Johnny..."

"Darb, go stem up twelve cents. We'll get a short dog and then hit those hotels, like I said. Okay?"

"G-gee. it's late for Restaurant. Ain't it?"

"Do like I say." The light pressed my eyes and I had to cover them, pushing against the closed lids. My stomach had begun to curl again. And it couldn't be for lack of wine. Not this quickly.

"Go, Darby, go. Don't stand there arguing."

He blinked and nodded, started off through the streaming foot traffic. Darby was a premier panhandler. His years in the ring had given him a smashed face and a shuffling grace that appealed strangely to more prosaic folk. His stutter and the bland innocence in the pale eyes, completed the picture of bumbling, honest poverty. He rarely braced a blank. In ten minutes he could beg more change than I in ten weeks.

That's how long it took him, ten minutes. He came back grinning and I knew he'd scored. He had a dime and five pennies in his thick hand.

"It's good today, Johnny," he said, pulling me out into the sidewalk crush. "I coulda got enough for both of us. Huh, Johnny? Can I?"

"No."

We fought the surge of walkers, moving slowly uptown. At the first corner, I turned, pulled Darby. He trailed me by a step, spouting a line of unintelligible commentary that I didn't bother to listen to.

The sun had poked through the overcast and a faint heat had come to the day. But here was no sun where my mood lay; I scraped my ruined shoes on the pavement, bumped people without thought of apology. A sign caught my eye and I fumbled the money into my hand and strode for it. If I'd been thinking better, it never would have happened.

"This one here, Johnny? Uptown?" Darby pulled on my arm, his eyes shuttling. "These people duh—d-don't like us b-buying in their places, Johnny."

"This one," I said, and turned in the glass-bricked doorway. "This one."

It was dim inside. And it smelled like fresh-cut cardboard. A customer at the counter had the salesman tied up. That's all that saved me. The salesman was a small man with thinning hair and bright, ferret eyes. He looked up at my entrance. There was a familiar grin on his face; a sort of wise half-grin. And it should have been familiar.

Barney.

"I'll be through in a minute, fella," Barney said, his voice cut through the smoke in my head. It was all I could do to keep from running to him. I dropped my eyes, turned for the door. "Hey, buddy," Barney called. "I said in a minute."

I ran. Plain ran. Outside, Darby greeted me with a storm of stuttering. I grabbed his arm and took off down Hill Street, leaving swirls of cursing people in our wake.

We got the bottle on Fifth. Like we should have done to begin with. Darby thought I'd gone crazy. I couldn't talk. Not for a long time. Barney. My friend, my schoolmate. To him I was a five dollar donation to the floral wreath racket, a plot in Greenbrier and a few warming memories.

When we did get the wine, Darby had to snatch it from me to keep me from drowning. Then we continued on our quest for food. The Tokay bounced in me, sending out smoky streamers of half-pleasure, half-nausea.

Restaurant, in wino language. is a term describing a short hustle. It goes like this: You beg enough food, from hotels, big restaurants and so on, to stack up a good spread. Then you invest a few cents in whatever it is you don't have. Usually bread. These eats are then hawked to the rest of the Brotherhood—or at least that portion which decides that this day they must eat. The store is a packing case in Nightmare Alley, a winding, dark cavern leading off Los Angeles street.

It's a gamble. For two reasons. One, you never know what you can get from those back doors; two, the winoes eat solid food seldom and if the day you pick is the wrong one, you're dead. Then you have no evening bottle. And to a wino, that's the one deadly fear.

Strangely, I did better at this particular begging than did Darby. Cooks took one look at my hollowed-out face, my sagging clothes, and ran for a piece of butcher's paper to wrap some kitchen scraps for me. I suspect they thought I'd fall dead on the doorstep without food—and quickly.

"How much have we got, Darb?" I placed a wrapped parcel I'd received at a bustling. chromed cafeteria in my friends' already loaded arms. "With this one, is it enough?"

"It's a lot, Johnny. A whole, whole lot." His brow wrinkled in concentration. "But we owe B-benny a quarter. Then we'll need at least four bits more ..."

I was feeling much better. I turned up the street. "Come on, then. We'll get this hotel and go find a spot in the alley."

It was a small hotel as big-city hotels go. And because of the district—two blocks from Civic Center—it was a busy one. A uniformed doorman stood ramrod-straight under the neat marquee. He was important. because the trades entrance was a small entryway right close to the main door. There was no alley behind this hotel. I stopped in a doorway, waved Darby up beside me.

"Doorman," I said. Darby nodded. "Turn him while I make the slop chute, there."

He arranged his packages, stuffing some inside the checkered jacket, then shuffled up the street. He stopped in front of the doorman, asked him something, sputtering on purpose. The doorman waved him away. Darby bobbed his head, a big silly grin splitting his face. The doorman said a word, probably a bad one, and retreated through the wide door.

I ducked down the slanting walk at the side of the building, heading toward the scullery door. It was lower than the street, the walk sloping steadily downward. A man in soiled whites had a hose on the garbage rack, washing huge cans. I pulled off my hat, walked up to him. The smell curling upward from the mess on the platform almost flipped my stomach.

"What do you want?" the man said, seeing me.

"Excuse me. Could I see the chef? Is he here?"

The man's little eyes. red-rimmed from the steam, swept my rags, came back to my bearded face. "No bums," he said, and went back to his garbage cans. The hose swooshed into a stinking tin, spewing water all over me.

I grinned at him. "I gotta see the chef. I'm not a bum. I'm a—a cook. Yeah, I'm a cook."

The little man dropped the hose, wiped his hands on his dirty apron. His eyes were less unfriendly now. "Cook?" He kicked the spouting hose aside. "Don't look like one."

I wiped the greasy water from my face, using a sleeve. My cheeks burned under the whiskers. I wanted to reach out and jerk the man off the concrete platform. But I remembered Darby and twisted my hat instead.

"I am," I said. "See if the chef'll see me."

The scullery man went into the kitchen, banging the door loudly behind him. It was a screen door, clogged with grease and pieces of lint. The smell of food came clearly to me and I realized just how long it had been since I'd eaten properly. Maybe I'd eat tonight. Instead of drinking. Then, if I could make it till morning, I could begin to taper off.

Then the cold question hit me. Why? For what? Taper off and what could I do then? I pushed my hands down into pants pockets. Both of them had holes. I waited.

"You want to see me?" A fat man in spotless white pushed on the screen, stood looking down at me.

"Yeah. I uh—you see, I'm a cook."

The scullery man squeezed past the chef, returned to his garbage rack. I could see his ears vibrating, listening to the conversation. The chef waited impatiently, a frown beginning on his florid face.

"Well, what I wanted," I said, "was something to eat. No use lying about it." I jerked a thumb at the scullion. "He wouldn't get you and I knew better than to ask him. So I told him I was a cook."

The chef said nothing. I ran a hand over my beard, let my knees buckle just a little. His eyes ran over my rags, returned to my face. The whole tour. Then he half-turned, saying over his shoulder, "Wait here."

The little weasel on the can rack laughed, high and nasty. I turned away, pretended an interest in the brick side wall, spattered with food stains and grease and gouged by delivery trucks. The hose hummed, thumping water into the cans under pressure. I just stared.

"Hey," a deep voice called. "Come here."

The chef stood in the doorway, a large bundle wrapped in a tom apron in his hand. He held it out.

"Put this under your coat." His eyes flicked to the scullion who turned hastily away. "Ain't supposed to do this. Too many beggars." He snorted. "Against the rules of the Hotel Thessaly. Mister Highpockets Henry, he thinks—"

I stopped him. "What did you say?"

"Huh? What did I—"

"The name of this place—what did you say it was?"

He looked at me, eyes narrowed. "The Thessaly. Hotel Thessaly. What'd you think it was, the Beverly Hilton?"

"No. No, not at all. I—" I pushed the bundle under my coat, thinking furiously. Thessaly. It had been so long. And just a mention. I jammed my hat on, pushed it back on my head. The chef's expression was understandably puzzled. "Look, I'm not crazy. It's just that I used to know a guy..."

The chef sighed. "Look, you got your lump. I don't want a story. So just beat it."

"Wait. Just one minute. One thing. Tell me, is the bell captain a guy named—" I fumbled in my tender mind, trying to remember. "Jerry? No, not Jerry. Barney, Barney—all I can think of is—wait a minute! Julius. The bell captain's name is Julius."

"You do this every place you go? Christ! So the boss hop's name is Julius. So what?"

He turned. I gripped his trouser leg with dirty fingers, leaving black smudges on the gleaming white.

"Wait. Look—could I see him? I mean just for a minute. Would you ask him if he'll see me?"

He didn't want to do it. But I talked, all of my sales glibness returning. I didn't stop to think why I was doing this thing. The answer wouldn't have helped. At last the chief agreed to see if the man, Julius, was on duty.

He was and he came, a little man, slick and natty; green-gold uniform plastered to a neat body, and wise eyes squinting in the half-light of the scullery entrance. He looked like a slightly overweight jockey. He skipped lightly down the steps, sauntered to where I stood by the side wall, and lit a long filter-tipped cigarette.

"Smitty said you wanted to see me. For what?"

I nodded, speechless suddenly. What did I have to say to this man? The wine I'd guzzled roared in me now, reaching its peak in the aroused excitement I felt. Why I was excited, I didn't take time to figure. Maybe I should have.

"I didn't mean to bother you," I muttered. Then, "Oh, hell. What I wanted was some information. You can give it to me. I can't pay you but it means a lot to me."

His old-young eyes watched me through the smoke from his cigarette. "What kind of information? I don't think I know you, friend."

"No, you don't." I stepped close to him, resenting the way his face twisted at my nearness. "A girl," I said, spitting it out. "Her name was Dee. I want to know where she lives."

There. It was out. My course of action, for win or for broke was set with the words. The wine would be no good from here on out. The little man blanked his face, pushed away from the wall.

"I don't read you, friend." His tone was off-hand, extra casual. "Dee's been out of action for a long time. Months. No good, anyway—too fussy. Sharp kid, but out of action." He took a step. "See you around, friend."

I said, "No," very gently. I gripped his thin shoulder. Not hard. A light began glowing behind my eyes. I tightened the grip. "Her address. Julius. That's all. No obligation. That's all. Then I'll leave."

"Hey, look, creep—get the hand off!" He twisted. I held, squeezed. "Look, fella, I said let go!"

He swung an elbow and it socked into my unprotected ribs. Breath whistled out my nostrils. I pulled him, my other hand grabbing the front of the bright uniform. Then I slammed him up against the wall, lifting his feet off the wet pavement. He wasn't talking now; he wasn't pushing at all. His little eyes slid and his mouth worked. Blood filled his dark cheeks.

It must have been a curious sight, at that. A ragged wino with a dirty beard, skinny and angular, exuding wine fumes and hot curses, hoisting the neat, uniformed body of the bell captain off the ground. I didn't know what I was feeling. Whatever it was, it burned. And he knew it.

"Wait, now," Julius said weakly. "Take it easy, friend." His heels scrabbled at the wall. My forearms felt rigid, like frozen wood. I pulled him away from the bricks slammed him back. I felt like I could put him through the wall if I wanted to.

He whimpered, his head snapping back. "Wait, now. Take it easy, for Christ's sake! I'll tell you, I'll tell you! I woulda..."

I let him down, feeling the tremble begin in my back, my legs. I rubbed a hand over my eyes.

"Write it," I told him.

He got a piece of paper, scribbled. I took it and turned to thank him, but he'd gone, dashing into the scullery door, one hand pulling at his disarranged uniform.

The wine roar was higher now, so, wrapping my hand around the piece of paper, I took off up the ramp. Three steps and I was running, loose soles slapping on the pavement like echoes from a distant past.

CHAPTER TEN

Darby thought I'd gone crazy. And maybe he was right. Within minutes of the Hotel Thessaly, we had stemmed forty-six cents between us, taken the Angel's Flight incline up to Bunker Hill and were looking for the address the bell captain had scribbled for me.

Brownstone fronts and old-style wooden houses squatted in pale afternoon sun. I moved along the sidewalk, shouldering pedestrians, searching the houses for the right number. Darby trotted along behind. His arms were still piled with packages. He didn't understand—but he followed.

My face was wet with sweat but the trembling had subsided somewhat. The thought of the girl, the hustler I'd met months before in the York Club, affected me strangely. I couldn't pin it down. Why should I be agitated? All right, so I'd had some wine. I was used to wine. Why the heaving chest bit and the blurred vision?

The house was converted frame, big and spreading, with bay windows, cupolas and a wide wooden veranda. It had four mailboxes on the front near the door. a name card under each. I could see a dark hallway through the elliptical glass of the door. No sign of life. The houses all around were cut from the same mold, and all were chopped into apartments. Private residences had long given up Bunker Hill.

"Is this it, Johnny? The house you wanted?"

I turned to him. I'd forgotten him. "Yeah, Darb. This is it. This is the place, Darby. This is the goddam place." And I laughed.

"Johnny, What's wrong? You're f-funny."

"I don't know, Darb. I don't know." I flopped on the worn steps, pushed my head into hot hands. My head ached. "I thought I knew for a minute there. I had it all. No doubts, no wondering. The whole thing figured out. Now—" I raised my eyes, looked at the concern in his battered features— "I don't know."

"You—you take it easy. I'll sit here and keep you c-company."

Something prodded my ribs. I dug inside the worn coat, pulled out the apron-wrapped lump the chef at the Thessaly had given me. Meat juice stained the outside. I looked at it; bounced it up and down in my hand. Why Dee? The least of my acquaintances in the old life. Maybe that was it. Maybe because she hadn't been a part of the Johnny Babcock that panted after a crown of chestnut hair, danced to the whimsey of a slit skirt.

I stood up suddenly and threw the package down the street as far as I could. I watched it hit and spill on the sun-soaked pavement.

"Johnny!" Darby wailed. He started up. I grabbed his jacket, pulled him back. "J-johnny, look . . ."

I said into his face, "Who am I, Darby? Look at me!" I shook him, pushed him back against the stairwell. "Tell me who I am!"

"Yuh-you're Johnny. Juh-Johnny . . ."

"Johnny," I said. I started that damn laughing again. But low this time, deep inside—swelling up out of the unidentified burn in my chest. "Johnny the hopeless. Johnny the joke."

"Wait, now, Johnny." Darby gripped my hand where it rested on his arm with a broken-knuckled hand. Gripped hard. His eyes, trying so hard to hold still, slid liquidly. He stammered. "Is t-this t-the house, Johnny? Is it a guh-girl, Johnny? Here, I mean?"

I leaned forward, the laughter stopping abruptly. My head rested on Darby's shoulder. I opened my mouth and breathed that way, trying to get some of the deadening wine fumes up out of me. Darby sat stiffly, afraid to touch me and afraid to move.

"Yeah, Darby," I said. "It's a woman. What else? What would she say if I walked in like this, huh? Can you imagine what she'd say—being a woman?"

"She might be glad. Johnny. M-maybe…"

"Glad!" I looked up at the house. She might be in there right now. "They're all the same, Darby. You take it from your uncle Johnny. All bad. They all stink."

"Nuh-no, now, Johnny. No they don't."

I started off, still unsteady on my feet. Darby skipped along behind me, steering me. He still tried to get it straight. He jabbered. But by now his wayward lips would accept no control at all.

We walked back down from Bunker Hill. I, more sober—Darby, more puzzled. He spoke just once.

"Johnny, what was h-her name? The girl's—back there?"

"Dee," I told him. "Her name was Dee. I knew her a long time ago. In another time. She's not important."

I looked at him. His face was turned away from me. He realized that he was violating the precept—the single factor that made our relationship possible, by asking questions. You couldn't call it a friendship. Friends are more demanding. If they can't know all your faults and have the generous, smug feeling of forgiving you for them, you're no good to them. Darby knew nothing of me, except what I showed in day to day relations. He seemed satisfied. I knew I was.

Until today. Today something had slipped. Maybe Darby had sensed the change and some of the restless what's-next feeling had rubbed off on him. I put my hand on his sturdy shoulder.

"Don't worry about Dee. It's long ago…" A surge of wine hit my throat; I swallowed like mad.

Darby grabbed my arm.

"Help me, Darb," I said, leaning on him. "Help me."

❧   ❧   ❧

Maggie St. Vincent Halloran had come to Los Angeles from somewhere in the corn country. A rather plain woman, with no distinguishing characteristics except a magnificent head of hair she swore had been pure white since high school, she had not followed Mr. Greeley's advice—rather Mr. Halloran's advance.

An itinerant printer by that name had stopped in the midwestern city where Maggie taught elementary school, long enough to envelope the aging and wistful spinster in his personal aura of romance, his permanent aroma of whisky and a whirl of activities which culminated in marriage. Sid Halloran had made life sing for Maggie. Not for long. But when the song ended, the haunting notes had lingered on.

Halloran left and Maggie followed. All she really knew of her wandering and charming spouse was that he would not be long in one place—nor long without a drink. She took her savings and began a five year odyssey in search of the wraith of Halloran. He was not a difficult man to trace; just hard to find. His name was indeed Halloran; he was a printer. And a union man. On these facts Maggie jumped from city to city in the Golden West, a week, a month, sometimes a mere stride behind the fast-moving linotypist. She never caught him, never found him.

But she found Los Angeles. And Fifth street. Through the tight-lipped, square-shouldered search for the man who had momentarily brightened her existence, she became aware of the many lost souls in the Brotherhood, and she came to love them. Nobody knew if this was her substitute for the late blooming love Halloran had brought her or merely a compassionate development of looking for her man in places where the Brotherhood congregated.

One of the few places in the country not at all affected by the global scramble was Skid Row. Higher wages meant nothing; the Brotherhood wouldn't work. A few drifted into the various services. But they were back soon, stemming, swiping hubcaps. The uniform services had no use for a man to whom no indignity was great enough not to be endured with a shy grin. During these years, Maggie had come to Los Angeles.

There was a small tavern on Fifth called the Trout House. It had gone out of business during the last months of the war. The name was an odd one and no one seemed to know just why it had been named the Trout House. But the name suffered a change, as did the tavern's fortunes from the time Maggie St. Vincent Halloran invested her tiny capital, infinite patience and incredible wiry strength in the defunct business. The location was terrible. A Mission on one side, a secondhand store on the other. And the Trout House seemed to incorporate the bad features of both. There was no neon, no fancy signs of any kind except some scraped paint on the front window.

That was the Doniker. And it was always crowded. All winos and border-line alcoholics. The Brotherhood of Bitter Wine. Headquarters, Los Angeles branch.

Everyone knew Maggie's personal history. She made a point to tell everyone; someone might run into Sid. There still remained, in her schoolteacher's heart, the remnants of a hope that someday Sid Halloran would come to Fifth street. If he did, she would be there. She ran the Doniker and she kept her financial head above water. No one knew how.

The original sign on the window still remained. Minus the two front letters. In peeling paint the sign now said, "The outhouse." Which became "The Doniker," naturally.

Darby's voice came to me: "Muh—Maggie wants you to come in the back 'n eat something."

I raised my head off the wooden bench far enough to peer upward at Darby. He had shaved. Maggie always made him shave. He wore a white apron and his cap and coat were gone. This was one of his working-for-Maggie periods.

"No," I said.

"Johnny, she said, M-maggie said—"

"I don't care what she said. Get away from me."

I was sitting on the floor. The sawdust was warm but not very clean. Somehow I'd fallen asleep with my head on one of the long benches along the sidewall of the Doniker.

"You got an appointment. Johnny. Remember?" Darby's big hands worked under my armpits, lifted. "Come on n-now, Johnny. Come on ..."

"Put me down." I had to move my feet as he propelled me toward the rear of the narrow room. The place was empty. It was very early morning. "What time is it?"

"Six-thirty. It's time to open up. The boys'll be wanting their wake-ups and short duh-dogs. You know Maggie never lets anyone sleep in the place, Johnny. You gotta get out of sight."

We pushed through the door in the rear. It was a combination kitchen and sleeping quarters; the only room other than the barroom. Maggie stood at the tiny stove in one corner, frying bacon and eggs. The odor almost made me retch. A plain, narrow cot, primly made, filled one corner. There was a table and Maggie's rocker. Nothing else. She turned as we entered.

"You're alive, John," she said. Her bright, black eyes ran over me. "Get him on the bed, Darby. And then go open up. And don't forget the beer case this morning."

"Yes 'm."

"And no drinking for you." She pointed the dripping spatula like a sword. "Mind, now, no credit for anybody unless you ask me."

Darby nodded, half-carried me to the cot. I flopped on it, still pretty foggy. The smell of blankets and clean sheets almost made me drunk all over again. Maggie made a clucking noise. Darby murmured and muttered, placing a piece of paper under my shoes, a rag under my dirty head. He started to go.

"Darb."

"Yes, Johnny?"

I rolled my head on the soft pillow. It seemed loose on my neck. I itched all over. This was always the way after a fall-down, dirty drunk. I tried to search my memory but everything was soggy and full of shadows.

"What'd you mean, I have an appointment?"

"The phone call, Johnny."

"What phone call?"

"Don't you remember the fight with Montrose? When he got mad 'cause we duh-didn't make anything day before yesterday?"

"Day before—" I groaned. "What's today?"

"Saturday."

"Tell me about the phone call."

"You called somebody. Your wife. You said …"

Then I remembered. It came rushing back and pinned me to the cot as returning memory slapped at me. Maggie told Darby to leave me alone and get out front. I barely heard the exchange. I was looking inward at the picture of a fool.

Montrose. We'd had a little argument. He incited my rage; the coal of resentment which had been burning since waking in the doorway. I remembered telling him I could get money. Not to pick on me about money. Did he think I was a lousy, wine-ridden, do-nothing like him—like the rest of them? The place had been full. Everybody drunk or drinking, the tiny radio filling the narrow room with recorded music. And that's all you could hear. The music and me.

Maggie stayed out of it. She seemed to sense that I was not striking out at Montrose. I didn't hit him. Just pushed him around a little. Then I called Edna from the drugstore on the corner, borrowing the money from Maggie.

The booth was small and smelly. Someone had whittled on the tiny phone table with a knife, gouging the edges, tracing initials on the flat surface. I called my home.

When the phone was answered finally, a voice I didn't know spoke. Edna had moved. Until that moment I had been pretty drunk. But suddenly, with no transition from the weakening alcoholic haze, I sobered. I'd forgotten that my dear wife had moved.

"You say Mrs. Babcock no longer lives there?"

"That's right," the pleasant voice said. "This is Mrs. Palmer. We moved in about a month ago."

"I see. Would you know where she lives now?"

"No, I'm sorry. We rent the house and I haven't seen Mrs. Babcock since we moved in."

"I see. What—I mean, how do you negotiate?"

"You mean the rent?" The woman-voice pounded in my ear. The headache had come back. With help. "We rent from A. L. Haggert. They're in the book."

She hung up. I called the Realtor and explained that I was a friend of Mrs. Babcock. Would they have Mrs. Babcock's number? They would and I called.

"Hello? Who is this?"

"Edna …" My tongue felt like pound of wet felt. For a long, breath-holding moment I could say nothing at all. The remembered tone, deep and insinuating, the peculiar pulsation of intimacy. "Edna. Edna, I—"

"Who is this? Now, look, whoever—" She stopped abruptly. Her breathing quickened, magnified by the telephone. "Johnny? Is that you?"

"It's me," I said. "Me, Johnny Babcock. Don't hang up, Edna."

"I won't," she said. Then the voice changed again, scaling downward. "But you'd better. You'd better hang up and go buy another bottle."

"With what? Edna, listen. I'm broke, I'm dirty … Edna, what are you doing to me?"

"Johnny, shut up." She took a breath. "Now, listen. I have nothing for you. Understand? You're dead, Johnny. And you'd better stay that way. I've kept track of you. I know what you've been doing. Go back to your wine and leave Edna alone." Her voice got hard. "Or you'll be real sorry, Johnny."

"Wait a minute." My voice had steadied. "You'd better know how things are. You've left me pretty defenseless, Edna. That's a mistake. A man does funny things when he thinks he has nothing to lose."

"Listen, buster. You just keep remembering that little room up in Quentin."

"'Oh, I remember that, all right. But there are things worse than death, Edna. Lots worse. You'd better listen to me."

She sensed the mood I was in. Her husky tones dropped, got the hint of intimacy again. "Go ahead. But make it quick. I've got an engagement."

"I'm happy for you. I've got one, too—with a cop."

"Johnny, now listen..."

"No. You listen. I got nothing much to lose anymore. I can't work and I'm afraid to steal. That means I get in trouble begging or laying around drunk." I paused. "Think about that a minute, Edna."

"What about it?"

"I might get arrested, Edna. How about that? What happens then?"

There was no answer. I could hear her breathing on the other end of the line.

"All right," she said, trying to the end. "What does that mean to me?"

"Oh, come on, for Christ's sake. You're smarter than that. And we both know it. You know if I get picked up I'm cooked. You think maybe I'll go alone?"

"They'd never believe you," she said quickly—too quickly. "Never. My word against yours. They'd—"

"They'd believe my fingerprints."

This time the silence lasted longer. Then she sighed, said, "All right, Johnny. How much? And remember how much we meant to each other, darling. A hundred thousand isn't all the money in the world."

"Save it. Where'll you meet me?"

"Poor Johnny. Poor old suburban Johnny." Her soft laugh purred in my ear. "Can't even make it as a wino."

The booth squeezed me. For a moment I couldn't see, couldn't hear. Then I gripped the receiver.

I said, "Look, bitch." My voice shook. "You get your ass down to Fifth, three blocks south of Main. Drugstore on the corner. I'll be outside. And you be here. Or you and me, we'll go sniff that happy pill together!"

Maggie's firm hand under my head pulled me back, shook the remembrance. The image faded. I opened my eyes, looked up. The woman's dark, compassionate eyes were fixed on my face.

"You've been groaning, John," she said. Her strong arm lifted me to sitting position. "Sit up. Drink this."

"Maggie. Maggie, when was it I borrowed the dollar? Was it last night?"

She held the thick cup filled with black coffee out to me. She said, "Drink this," and I took it. Then she said, "No, John. Not last night. Night before last. Thursday. You said you wanted to call your wife."

"Night before last! But what—" I groaned, pushed the cup back into her hands.

"Here. Stop that. Sit around here and stop feeling sorry for yourself."

I turned, sullen now, and resentful even of this small kindness. The cup was hot and it felt good in my hands when she made me take it. But I couldn't drink the stuff. Two days. Where had they gone? Maggie had some wine in the kitchen, I knew. But I didn't ask for any. Something stopped me. Something I wasn't yet ready to put a name to.

"Tell me about yesterday."

"Drink the coffee."

I pretended to sip.

Maggie, small and quick-moving, wearing a pressed and starched sweatshirt, that she made look like a middy blouse, and a tweed skirt. It's what she always wore. With low-heeled shoes and dark stockings. A small woman, with tiny hands and an unlined face dominated by the great, staring, dark eyes. She moved to the rocker, sat on the edge of the seat.

"You lost yesterday, I guess." She smiled fleetingly. "It was yesterday you had the appointment."

"Why didn't I keep it?"

"You did. Or so you said."

I'd seen Edna. And I didn't even remember it.

"I don't remember," I said wonderingly. "I just don't remember. Anything. Except the phone call. Then nothing." I turned to the small woman. "Nothing, Maggie. Nothing!"

She nodded. "It happens. You met a woman in a big car down on the corner. Brassmouth saw it. Then you came here with a handful of money and shoved it in Montrose's face."

"How much? What did I do with it?"

"Close to five hundred dollars. I've got it. I'll keep it for you."

"What happened then?"

"You got pretty drunk. Real drunk." She put her fingertips on her smooth face, turned away. "And a little nasty, John. I'm sorry to say."

I dipped into the coffee, sucked it up without thinking. Maggie looked at me for a long time. When she spoke, her voice was faint and tinged with something like fear.

"I let you sleep here last night, John. The one rule I've never broken before."

"I know," I said. "Why?"

"Because," she said, sighing, "I was afraid to let you go out. Afraid you'd be killed."

I drank all of the coffee then.

CHAPTER ELEVEN

"Here's what happened," Maggie said. "Yesterday, after you left on your tear, two men came here and asked for you."

"Asked for me?"

"Yes. For a tall, thin fellow with a black beard named Johnny."

"Just Johnny?"

She looked up. "That's all. They were pretty well dressed. One looked like he might have been a Mexican. We told them nothing, that we didn't know you or know of you."

"Did you get their names?"

Maggie rose, walked to the small stove. She poured a cup of coffee and brought it back to me. I took it.

"Maggie, forget it."

"These weren't the kind of men who leave cards." Maggie took the rocker again, sat facing me. "But I've seen enough of their kind since I've been here to recognize them. They were hoodlums. And they wanted you."

"I'd better leave. Take the money and leave."

"Maybe. But I hate to see you letting it whip you." She leaned forward. "John, you know I don't pry. But I've got to tell you something."

"Maggie, forget it."

The slight woman bent forward in the rocker. Her legs, modestly encased in the dark hose, were held together and the small, strong hands lay in her lap.

"You'd better fight now, John. If you've got something to fight. It gets harder the longer you put it off."

"Maggie, you don't know anything about it."

"And I don't want to. I only know you. That you don't belong here—on Fifth street. You're not the type. I don't care why you're here. But I care about you. Oh, don't ask me why. I care about all of you."

I fell back on the covers. "Get out of here. Get out, and leave me alone."

Her voice continued, beating through my hands locked over my ears.

"Don't run, John. You've been running long enough. And you're not the running kind. Stop and face it."

"Yeah. Yeah, that's real pretty." I sat up again. "Maggie, get me a drink."

"Not now."

I fell back, pressed my face against the pillow. I said, "What do you mean, not now? I got money. I can—"

"Johnny, Johnny..." She sat on the edge of the cot; I felt her weight, her warmth. The clean smell of her offended me. Like new laundry. "Listen, John. This is no joke. Your friends are worried about you."

I laughed, twisted. "My friends. You should bottle that and sell it. I don't want any friends. I had some. All I want is a drink."

The main room door opened and Darby entered. He left the door ajar and the sound and the odor from the bar washed in. The babble and the stink. I looked down at my ruined clothes. My clothes! George Carter's clothes. What a big laugh that would be for him if he knew. We had traded places, all right. And maybe he did know.

Darby wrung his hands in the apron he wore, looked at me. There was something odd in his eyes; something I'd never seen before. They shuttled, like always, and he stammered. But there was something else.

I said, "Take it easy, Darb. Easy. Slow it down."

His sliding grin came. I noticed that his face was slicked with sweat and his feet moved all the time. Even when he was standing still.

"Muh-Maggie," he said, his eyes flicking from the woman's face to mine. "There's a guy wants a short dog tuh—t-til late this afternoon. What should I do?"

"Who?"

"Buh-Billy Jameczek and that fella they call Bootnose. Yeah, Bootnose."

Maggie nodded. She pointed at me. "You don't tell anyone where he is. Right?"

"Oh, no, sir, Maggie. No s-sir." He bobbed his head. His tongue came out, washed dry lips. He tried to say something but the lips wouldn't behave.

"It's okay, Darb. Everything. You understand?"

He swallowed, nodded. He went out quickly. A roar from the assembled winos greeted him.

I sipped the coffee and tried to think. But nothing made any sense. All of a sudden my safe little rose-tinted world was all messed up. The coffee warmed the chill in my gut and cleared my head. I looked at Maggie.

"Montrose said you had a job for me. Playing piano?"

She shrugged. "That was days ago. It doesn't seem very important, now. You want something to eat? Or are you going to continue drinking?"

"I don't know, Maggie. Don't nag me."

"All right. But the wine is no good any more. Can't you see that? Not for you."

"It's always good," I muttered.

"No it isn't. And you know it. You've come to the point where you're going to do something about—about whatever it is that troubles you. As I said, you're not a runner."

"Built for distance," I murmured.

Maggie took the cup from me, went to the stove.

I said, "These men, Maggie. How did they know where to come?"

"All I know is what I've told you. Tell me about the woman in the car. She the one from Bunker Hill?"

"How did you know about that?"

"Darby was with you, remember?"

"Darby. I'll pound his—"

"Of course you won't!" The schoolteacher voice stopped me. Maggie marched over in front of me, stood hands on hips. "Now you listen to me, young man. That Darby thinks you're absolutely the whole world and a half acre of Texas. He wouldn't do anything to hurt you. Now, how about the girl?"

"No. It wasn't the same girl."

"The trouble is with your wife? The big trouble?"

"Yes."

"And the other—the girl on Bunker Hill—would she help you?"

"The girl on—No. No, Maggie, forget about that." I pulled my feet under me. "No help there. Besides, I'll never put my life into the hands of a woman again."

The white head moved back and forth. Maggie's eyes pitied me, I could see it. Her smooth, fine-porcelain skin crinkled around the eyes.

"One woman," she said softly, "is not all women. You are a fool."

"Granted. But I got over it."

She looked at me for a long time. I didn't turn away. She walked to the cupboard, got a bottle of cheap red wine out of it and brought it to me. She set it on the floor near the cot.

"I said are a fool." She started out of the room. "You stay here. Whatever those men want they'll not get in here."

I said, "Maggie, wait."

She stopped. I licked my lips, squeezed my eyes closed to marshal thought. "There's something wrong here. Suddenly it's a big turmoil and things are happening. I'm concerned about you. About Darby."

"Are you?"

"Of course. I don't want to be the cause of anyone else getting hurt."

"Anyone else?"

"Listen. I'd better get out of here. Get clear away."

"Go somewhere you're not known, is that it?"

I nodded, dropped my eyes. After a pause, she said, "If you say so. A man calls his own shots. There's one thing ..."

"What?"

"Darby. Did you notice anything about him? The way he acted?"

"Yes. Yes, I did. He's all shook, like. What's wrong?"

"He hasn't had a drink since you went haywire. Says he won't until you don't need him anymore."

She went out and closed the door.

At ten o'clock the Doniker was crammed. Saturday night. I'd slept the day away. The bottle of wine was still unopened on the floor. I was paying for that. Stomach flutter, nausea. An hour or so of dry heaves. And a real cottony headache. I lay on the cot and cursed myself for a fool. Drinking my way into oblivion; waiting for an unknown axe to fall.

The backroom, and my thoughts, became intolerable after a while. I went into the bar. It was full of blue smoke and growling conversation. And piano. Someone was tinkling Maggie's new piano. It was an old Haven-hurst upright with no top. At least one key was dead, my ear told me. Maggie and Darby worked behind the high, old-fashioned mahogany bar. The license called for beer and wine. But precious little beer was dispensed over the ancient wood. Behind the bar, a three-section mirror, old and yellow and wavery, divided by upright Doric columns of burnished wood, reflected the ragged crowd. The Brotherhood was happy tonight.

"Hello, Johnny. Have a drink."

Montrose and Bill Jameczek greeted me when I entered, washed and momentarily feeling better for the long sleep. I refused the drink offer, wandered through the long, narrow room, listening, watching. Darby caught my eye, grinned from one bent ear to another. His heavy shoulders rolled with pleasure when I worked up a weak smile for him in return. Maggie shook her head with disapproval, motioned toward the back room. I said nothing, did nothing. She went back to dispensing her wine and wisdom.

"Hello, Johnny," a slurred voice said at my shoulder "They tell me you been hard to hold lately."

Modesty Davis. I said, "I guess so. How you doing, Modesty?" Modesty was not a wino, strictly speaking. He had been. Now he'd gone respectable and worked every day somewhere. A woman in the picture, everyone said. But he still managed to get to the Doniker a couple of days a weeks, looking out of place in his neat clothes and clean face.

"Want a drink, Johnny?"

"No, Modesty. Not now. Thanks."

He shrugged, weaving back to the bar. I found a seat on the bench opposite the bar and flopped there. I felt loose, boneless— like one of those dolls you buy whose joints are tied with pieces of string. My stomach clutched and rolled, and the beard itched. I leaned my head against the wall, closed my eyes and let the noise and smell, the social feeling of people together, wash over me.

The piano stopped with a sudden discord.

I opened my eyes. The pasty-faced man had fallen forward over the keys. Darby hurried from behind the bar to remove the man from his draped position on the keyboard. Everyone roared for an encore. The man had passed out like a light in the middle of a number.

Modesty turned at the bar. "Johnny plays piano, boys. Maggie told me so. Hey, Johnny …"

He started toward me. I shook my head in protest but the cry had been taken up through the whole room. Montrose stuck his silken beard in my face.

"Come on, boy," he said. There was no rancor in his voice or manner. He had forgotten our little trouble. "Come. Your public waits."

"I'm sick, Monty." I shook off his hand. "Tell them."

I looked at Maggie and she suddenly got busy, sweatshirt flashing in rapid motion behind the plank. A pint bottle waved under my nose. The fruity odor sank into my brain like a whiff of ammonia. I pushed it away, got up.

"Come on, Johnny," Modesty said. His color was high and he smelled like Fifth Street in the morning. His woman would give him hell tonight. Or the other way around. "Come on and play for us. Darby's been bragging all day how Johnny was gonna play tonight."

The pushing hands and helping shouts got me to the piano. I sat down. The keys seemed terribly close together.

Someone shouted, "Play!" and I played. Chopsticks. The room applauded extravagantly. Then I cracked my fingers, took the well-remembered limbering exercises and quit clowning. I played the Warsaw Concerto. Better than I'd ever played it in my life, or so it seemed.

The audience was a strangely attentive one. They listened politely and intelligently and they never knew what it did for Johnny Babcock. That's who played. Johnny Babcock. I banged the keys in welcome.

At first my fingers were stiff. It had been almost six months since I'd touched a keyboard. But the early dedication, before Europe and before Edna, paid off. I played the simple standards interspersed with a jazz theme or two, a couple of the better known classics. The Brotherhood approved. Gradually, as the spell of the music soothed the jumping of my nerves and laid the ghosts in my mind, an element of peace came to me. I'd had no peace in a long, long time.

"Johnny." Darby stood by the piano. "I buh-bought you a cold beer. A real cold one. You drink it, Johnny."

"I'm not drinking, Darb. Thanks." I looked at the keys, swept over them with my fingers. "Like you."

"But the b-beer, Johnny. It'll help you. It's only the wine that's buh-bad. You drink it, Johnny. Please..."

I finished the number and stopped. A patter of applause and a few drunken cheers drifted in the smoke. Maggie looked up from the bar, face flushed. She shouted, "Play Melancholy Baby," and everyone hooted. I plunked out the Dragnet theme notes and brought down the house.

"The beer, Johnny."

"All right." I took the beer, punched him lightly on the shoulder. "Thanks."

It was cold and it was good. The bottle, wet from contact with ice, felt like a direct line to Alaska. I rubbed it in my beard, letting the coldness and moisture work some of the hard lines out of my face.

"Is it good, Johnny?" Darby waited eagerly for my reaction. Maggie called for him and he skittered, waiting. "Is it?"

"The greatest," I said. "And so are you, kid. Go to work. Who's going to play for you if you hold up the musician? And you got to buy breakfast. If we don't drink, we got to eat. Right?"

"Right." His fighter's body turned smoothly. "You play, Johnny," he said and went off, bobbing his head.

I played. The night flew by. One by one my public drifted out as various tolerances were reached. To doorways, to parked cars. To packing cases and storm sewers. The music changed and the place emptied and Johnny Babcock, back aching and forearms stretched from the unaccustomed playing, poured his troubled soul into a battered upright piano in a Skid Row bar with an audience of lost men and one hopeful woman.

Montrose said goodnight to me before he stumbled out. "Very good, John. But then I knew you would be, somehow. I've heard the best in the halcyon days—Horowitz, Arthur Rubinstein. You're good. I, uh—have a bit of the route change left." His rheumy old eyes squinted as he dug in a pocket. "If you'd like to take a little ..."

"No, Monty. Thanks."

He left. Modesty stumbled over, invited me to see him later about going to work. I thanked him. Maggie came by on her way to the room in back. She quit a little early, around one, leaving the closing up and cleaning to Darby. She smiled. Her powder-skin face was tired but the dark eyes had not lost the inquisitive sparkle, the compassionate light.

"Wonderful, John," she said. "Just wonderful. Hold it where you got it. The future is always fearsome, but it comes one day at a time."

"Thank you, Betty Bromide," I said, sending my fingers over the keys in a pastoral effect.

She laughed outright. "You and Darby sleep here tonight. Never mind the floor till morning. 'Night."

I nodded and she left.

Then there was no one but Darby and Me. Capitals. Like a book title. He wiped up the bar, took a chair by the piano and looked up at me in the low light. His thick shoulders hunched and there was less movement to his face and eyes than I had ever seen. My fingers were loose, now, and oddly agile. Like playing golf after a long lay-off; occasionally you shoot a fantastically good game the first time out. My mind built musical structures and my fingers flew over the keys. Chords grew and echoed in the small room. Darby watched and listened. His lips grew still.

"No fights tonight, Darb."

"No fights, Johnny." He blinked once, steadied. "I'm glad. I don't like fights. They said I wouldn't fight a baby after the operation, Johnny. Isn't that funny, fight a baby."

"Yeah. Who wants to fight a baby?" I grinned for him. My eyes were tired; the tendons in my forearms ached. But I didn't want to stop. I didn't ever want to stop.

"In fact, Darby," I said, raising my voice over a series of block chords hammered out by my resurrected fingers, "who wants to fight at all, huh? We're going to be all right, kid. You and me."

There was no answer. He was looking toward the door.

I looked, twisting on the stool. My hands stumbled, stopped. Notes hung discordant in a perfect silence, then dissolved like aspirins in hot water.

Two men stood in the doorway. As I looked, they stepped in, closed the door, locked it. One wore a grey topcoat. Both stood just within the pool of light from the one strip of neon which illuminated the room. All the other lights had been turned off.

They stood quite still, examining the room with searching eyes. Topcoat stepped forward. The other was slim, and seemed young; he wore a leather jacket, trimmed at the collar with fur. Both wore hats pulled low.

They didn't belong on Fifth Street. Unless they had business. And I knew at the first look what their business was.

Trouble.

CHAPTER TWELVE

They moved quietly and expertly, not speaking. I just sat there. Darby mewled deep in his throat, like a young animal in danger. Topcoat walked down the bar, eyes shadowed by his hat, one hand sliding along the bulge of the bar. His companion, smaller and more lithe, circled, moving warily. Under his leather jacket he wore well-cut expensive looking slacks and brushed suede shoes so blue they looked black. A wedge of narrow chin stuck out beyond the hat shadow.

I said, "You fellas looking for someone? We're closed."

Leather Jacket sniggered. The big one threw him a look, stopped at the end of the bar, a few feet from the piano platform. He spread his legs, distributed his considerable weight evenly. His gaze swung from me to Darby and back. He lifted his face, exposing a three-quarter profile of unrelieved brutality. A finger-wide scar began at one ear, ran across both lips diagonally and petered out at the chin bone. The eyes were deep-set and close together, with a dull shine to them.

"Which one 'o you's Johnny?" The mutilated lips did not move when he spoke.

I said nothing; Darby couldn't. Nobody moved. The big man ran his eyes over me, then turned to Darby again. Darby moved back to the wall, his hands raising in front of him as if to ward off a blow. His eyes shuttled.

"You," the big man said, pointing a finger at Darby. "Supposed to be a guy works here named Johnny. Who is it?"

The other man spoke; his voice was high-pitched, with a wild flavor. "Hey, Eddie. Like the guy on the—"

"I didn't ask you, Weddo. Keep an eye on the David Harum at the piano."

He took a step toward Darby. The apron had caught his eyes. I pushed away from the keyboard, stood up. The big man asked Darby a question and Darby whined and crouched lower. The man turned his back on me. He walked closer to Darb, cocking his right arm. Topcoat shifted his weight like a fighter, dug a whistling right hand under Darby's upraised arms. It crunched solidly and Darby screamed like a woman. Probably he was living it all again. All the cuts and the stitches; bloody bedsheets and sweaty anger, bones grating and senses whirling from battering, battering. There was no fight in him. Not anymore. He'd spent it all in smelly clubs in a thousand night-hung towns where the only real fight was between the manager and the promoter to see who stole the fighter's purse.

"Leave him alone," I said. "Leave him alone, you freak!"

I jumped off the platform. Months of wine and no food had weakened me. I would have had trouble with Tom Thumb. But I went ahead. Topcoat was whaling on Darby. He turned, cursing; I hit him flush in the mouth and his split lips popped bright blood.

"Leave him alone, leave him alone…" I muttered and punched, landing light blows on the big man's head and body. I'd lost sight of Leather Jacket.

Darby slumped to the floor. I could see his eyes, fear-filled and wild, peering from between his arms. I stood, breathing heavily while the man in the topcoat wiped a hand across his lips, pushing me away. He looked at the blood, cursed harshly. He lunged at me. I fell back against the bar and stuck out a foot. The sawdust swirled as the big body thumped on the floor, sliding. The other one, the slim kid, came around the piano, across the platform. He crouched there, springy and lithe, light striking the leather jacket and turning the folds blood red.

"Me, now, Eddie?" His tongue flicked out. "Want I should get him? You didn't do so good, Eddie. The broad'll never pay the other half this way."

He laughed. The big one cursed and kept cursing, getting up from the floor. I looked back to the slim kid; he had a bright length of bicycle chain in his right hand. He swished it against his slacks and looked at Eddie.

"What do you say, Eddie? You said not here. But I don't know, man. I don't know..."

The bar was at my back. The two men blocked the other directions. There was nowhere I could go. And they meant to kill me. I knew that now.

"Listen, you guys. Whatever she paid—" I gripped a chair for support. "Listen..."

"No listen," Eddie said. "There ain't no listen." He moved forward, like a lumbering truck in low gear. His twisted face was streaked with blood from his mouth. I hit him right in the middle of the smear, dredging up strength out of my fear. He fell, screaming, "Belt him, Weddo! Belt the wino sonofabitch!"

The thin one laughed. "It's a cinch, Eddie. Watch this, Eddie..." He crouched above me.

There was no use waiting for it. I spun the chair with one hand. It slid through sawdust, hit Eddie. I jumped at the other one, got one foot on the platform. The chain whizzed and slammed against my head.

Christ, it hurt! I've had shrapnel, broken bones, cleat wounds—nothing had ever been like that string of steel links swung by the laughing fool in the leather jacket. The first blow ripped over my ear, across my back. I threw up my hands, bent over. The big man came up on my right and crashed a chair over my back and the floor came up at me. I fell, sat dizzily. The kid jumped off the platform, wound up like a pitcher and wrapped the chain all the way around my head. The end popped my cheekbone like an eggshell. I screamed then. Leather Jacket laughed, high in his throat, and yanked on the chain. It pulled, and skin and flesh came with it.

I turned away, trying to call out. I met a foot propelled by the big man. It slammed against my shoulder, rocked me over on my back. I lay against the bar, huddling where the wood joined the floor. The big one kicked me in the back and consciousness faded, came back. He kicked me again. My eyes were closed and I could hear. I could still hear when I should have been dead. The babble became words, then individual voices.

"We can't finish him here, Eddie."

"Shut up."

"Someone'll come pretty soon, Eddie. Someone'll come. Too much noise, man."

"Shut up, Weddo, hear? Shut up."

For a moment there was nothing. Then the big one knelt beside me, lifted my head.

"Christ!" he said.

A high-pitched laugh sifted through my fog. The thin one burbled in glee. "Did I get him for beltin' you, Eddie? Did I get him? Is that cold, man?"

"Shut up, Weddo. Listen." The big man got up. "We're in trouble. We ain't got no time." His voice faded; I strained to keep from sinking into the bed of tar that invited and taunted me. "You're right, someone'll be here quick."

"Lemme stick him."

"No. Listen. Here's what we got to do. We kill him here. Beat him to death."

"With the chain, huh, man? I get it..."

"No. Not with the chain. Fists. Chairleg—something. We kick the dummy there a couple of times, mess him up. Then we leave 'em both. You get the bit?"

Somebody turned me over. A glimmer of light came through one eyelid although my eyes were closed. Pain returned with the movement.

"The dummy looks like a pro, Eddie," the high voice said. "The dummy. Maybe I'll need the blade, huh, man?"

"How do you know?"

"The nose, man. See it? I wonder what happened to his guts?"

"Wine," Eddie said. "And put the blade away. Just do like I say."

His face came down over mine. Through the slit in the eyelid I could see his expression, hard and jumpy and a little wild. This wasn't going according to the script and he didn't like it. I watched sweat bead heavily on his forehead, slide to mix with the blood on his chin. He grabbed the front of my shirt, lifted. He muscled me upright and the crazy kid chattered in the background.

"Get him up here. Eddie. Lemme have him, Eddie." The wild flavor of the kid's voice chilled me through the storm of pain. I tried to move but Eddie's rough hands moved me easily. He supported me with one thick arm. I wanted to cry out but there was no energy in me, only puzzling awareness. Everything was as clear to me as if I stood off somewhere and watched in three-dimensional clarity.

They plunked me in a chair. I couldn't see Darby, though I could hear him. A snuffling whimper from the floor.

Weddo said, "We gotta hurry, man. We gotta hurry. This ain't tappin' no till, man. This is the digger if the nabs come now."

"Shut up you goddam spic! Just be quiet and leave the thinking to me."

For a moment I thought the big man would hit the other. He was all wrought up. They glared, nose to nose. Then the slim kid backed away, muttering.

Eddie nodded, said, "Get behind this guy. Hold him." snapping my head back over the chair top. "Hurry,

"All right, Eddie." I felt rough hands on my throat, snapping my head back over the chair top. "Hurry, man."

Eddie hit me. A full arm swing flush on my already damaged face. And he knew how to hit. White worms wiggled out from the point of impact and converged at the back of my head. The pain was so bad I didn't feel it. Shock waves flowed in my twisted body. Then he turned and hit me again. I could hear the thin one chortling with every blow, pulling on my neck. Another smash tore my head from his grasp and I fell to the floor, feeling no impact. I felt packed in cotton. They hauled me erect, held me while the beating went on. Each blow became an impersonal drop of rain on a high, high roof.

They were killing me and I couldn't move a muscle. I couldn't even faint.

What happened then was hazy and flashing, all mixed up with blood-red spurts and sucking hurt and the belly-lurch of cold fear. But I saw most of it. The kid in the leather jacket cried out to Eddie to turn around. Eddie spun, topcoat swirling out with the motion. Darby had risen.

Darby Danbury came off the wall shuffling, bobbing his head. His eyes were narrowed, still. Shoulders hunched, he walked up to the big man, stuck out a left hand almost playfully. Eddie pawed at the big fist, stepping forward. Darby almost tore his head off with a right hand to the throat. I heard the dull thunk of the blow through my cotton batting.

The other, Weddo, jumped on Darby's back, a bright shard of blade glinting in his hand. I tried to give warning, to rise and tear this killer from my friend's back. I couldn't move. The thin kid struck; the licking blade disappeared into the muscle under Darby's right arm. Darby shrugged mightily and the kid flew over the bar, tumbling cases and breaking glass.

There were shouts, then, and the mad scrambling of a deadly serious fight between men who knew what fighting was about. The two thugs probably could have licked any one man in the world in a rough-and-tumble that night. Except Darby Danbury. Something had happened to the shuffling, grinning, loose-lipped man with the shifting old-young eyes. The only sound he made was a grunt with the effort of every devastating punch he threw.

He stalked the killers, hooking, jarring. And finally his grim advance brought panic.

The thin one tried to run, to get away from this implacable destroyer; Darby dropped him with a thrown chair. Then he caught big Eddie by his flaring coat, yanked the grey material to shreds.

Eddie, face almost unrecognizable, hair matted and bloody, stumbled back. He backed to the far wall, could go no farther. A bench caught his knees, half-buckled them. Darby glided up to him, right arm hanging uselessly. He set, rocked the big hood with a left from way down and hit him with the same hand again before he fell. The knife handle protruded from his shirt as if it had grown there; the arm hung, fist clenched still.

The left hand was more than enough.

Somewhere I got the strength to dig my face out of the sawdust. I leaned on the platform fighting the rising waves of blackness. I'll never forget what I saw. Darby, his face bleeding and expressionless, his shirt torn and stained black with blood, stood there and sent blow after crushing blow into the unresisting body of the man who had tried to kill me. Outside, a whistle blew. Close. Then I heard a siren's alley-cat wail growing in the night.

Maggie, fully dressed, came from the back room. She had run and called the law, I knew. I tried to get up, tried to get to Darby to stop him. I couldn't. My face leaked blood so fast the floor around me was a pool.

Weakly I called, "Darby! Darby, stop ..."

Somehow I got it out; weak and pitiful, but loud enough. And then it all ran out and everything came and went, nothing still, nothing solid. As if I whirled on the end of a burning string, climbing hand over hand as the flame ate upward.

Darby turned at my call. He stood for a moment, the deadly purpose draining from his rock-hard face. He came across the floor like a man wading in hip-deep water. He looked down at me.

All he said was, "Johnny. Gee, Johnny..."

Then he collapsed, falling forward over me and his weight hit me like a falling cloud.

When I woke the first time, I hurt all over. That's all I was conscious of—the hurt. The place was full of uniforms. Maggie had my head in her lap; I remember the laundered smell of her through all the hassle. I tried to ask her what had happened to Darby. I couldn't manage a word. The black rolled up in my brain.

I woke up to stay in a bright room. clean-smelling and sunny, with a radio playing softly somewhere and smooth sheets around me. One eye didn't operate at all. I sensed that my face was covered with bandages. I couldn't move to find out. My limbs didn't belong to me at all—nothing did. My sight was shaky, weak; images paled and colors wouldn't hold still for classification.

A shadow crossed the window, dimming the sun. A sharp, clean smell came to me, like stacked hay in a summer field, with just a suggestion of flowers. The shadow bent over me, its mouth moving with unheard words, its hands touching the mound of wrappings and covers. It was a woman, her silhouette trim and youthful. I blinked, the colors rushing, then fading out again. Then sight came back in a flood, like a television picture suddenly brought to focus.

It was Dee. It was strange how familiar the pale, heart-shaped face with the slanting eyes was to me. I'd known her so fleetingly. For a confused, reborn moment, I was happy. Just to see her again. To see anyone who had—

The import of the moment hit me suddenly. She was Dee.

She knew Johnny Babcock.

And Johnny Babcock was supposed to be very expensively dead.

CHAPTER THIRTEEN

The first week was a shifting, ever-painful haze of discon-
nected voices and sounds, needle pricks and occasional
flashes of lazy aloofness. Dee was my benefactress. It hadn't been
a dream. This was her Bunker Hill apartment. My bruised lips
would not handle words, even had I been willing to speak to her.
And I was not, for reasons I could not, in my confusion, discover.
I suffered her ministrations in total silence, even turning away
when she entered the room. Somehow she had become the focus
of all my anger, all my unreasoning resentment. She sat with me
for long afternoon hours, hands quietly folded in her lap, trim
body held erect, waiting for a sign from me. I gave none.

After the first awakening I could distinguish sounds. Soon,
every time she spoke the words came to me. But I never answered.
Some tight core of stubborn hurt held my tongue. There were
many things I wanted to know. But I could wait. I'd become
pretty good at waiting.

The doctor, a clean, antiseptic young man with blunt hands
and a rough way with a needle, came several times. He had taken
stitches in my face where the chain and the knuckles had ripped.
He had set the broken rib. I spoke to him from time to time—
explaining the pain, asking for an estimate on how long I'd be
laid up. This last he never answered satisfactorily.

"I can't say, Mr. Hanley—" this was the name Dee and Maggie
had dreamed up for me— "Except that when you start helping
out, the time will come sooner. You're not hurt that badly."

"What do you mean, Doctor?"

"You don't seem to want to get well, for one thing. Oh, I know, you've heard that tired cliché so many times." He bent over, tugged with deft roughness at the bandages on my face. "That doesn't remove the fact that it applies to you. The physiological healing is rapid; you seem to be an extremely healthy young man. Aside from being too thin and a trifle run-down."

I struggled up, put my back against the pillows Dee had arranged for me earlier.

"What about my face, Doc? I can feel stitches pulling under the bandages. Is it bad?"

He turned, began arranging the instruments he had used in the gaping bag on the bedside table. His quick, blunt hands never faltered.

"Yes," he said, "it's bad. That weapon—what was it, a chain?—Yes, well, that chain tore quite deeply. At first the damage will appear more fearsome than it really is. A cosmetic operation will fix some of it." He finished with the bag and stood relaxed beside the bed, young and frowningly pompous. "I did the best I could with those wounds. The one in the eyelid will heal completely, I'm sure of that. The others..." He shrugged.

"When can I get up?"

"Any time. Your rib is well taped. I'd like to get a picture of that. But I understand you would rather not go to a hospital. That's up to you." He snapped the bag shut, lifted it to the floor. "Move carefully for a week or so. The eye bandage can come off whenever you're ready. The lids will be stuck. Superation, nothing to worry about. A little rinsing in a warm boric solution will clean it up. I'll leave some. And next week, come to my office. I'll remove most of the stitches."

He tucked the end of his narrow, small-figured tie under his coat, picked up the bag. He looked at me intently, as if memorizing my face. He shook his head.

"You won't be back, Doctor Long?" Dee's voice invaded the room. She had entered quietly from the kitchen and stood, still wearing a pert pillbox of a hat and a coat thrown cape fashion over her shoulders. "This is the last visit?"

The young man turned, his face lighting up. She did look good. Her face had a warm color from climbing the stairs, and her tiny, perfectly proportioned body showed to advantage in a small-waisted cotton thing of lime and white. She looked cool, womanly.

The Doc said, "Dee. I didn't think you were going to come before I left."

She smiled at him. A funny, constrained sort of smile. "Here I am."

"Yes. And now you'll have to come to me. I've done all I could here." He walked toward her, carrying the squat bag. "With or without laughing boy, here."

"John, I—" She looked at me, trying to read my expression through the yards of gauze. I saved her the trouble by turning away.

"Yes, yes," the doctor said. "I understand. You could acknowledge the favor, however."

She murmured something. They walked into the front room together, voices muting. I lay back on the stacked pillows and breathed deeply. My rib hurt just a bit when I moved. I touched my face—the part the wrapping didn't cover—and marveled for the hundredth time at its odd feeling. The beard was gone, of course, and the area near the broken cheekbone was numb.

Thoughts flitted through my head, were gone before I could classify them. I felt drained, completely incapable of the most simple moves. Bits of the frantic few moments in the Doniker came to me and I was aware that the same impressions had come before. The drugs I'd been under had made the memories bearable for a while.

Women's voices trilled in the corridor and Maggie Halloran came into the room, striding purposefully. Dee trailed the small woman, her face a study in apprehension. She had removed her coat but the saucy hat still clung, as if defying gravity, to the piled mass of brown hair.

"How are you, John?" Maggie said, nodding shortly. She stopped at the bedside, looked down at me. "I didn't want to come before. How do you feel? Well enough to do something?"

I grinned, feeling the pull of sutures. My one eye had difficulty with depth and I missed her hand when I reached for it. She took it in hers, held strongly. "You got me out, didn't you?"

"Yes."

Maggie wore a cloth coat over the familiar pink sweatshirt and tweed skirt. Her feathered white hair gleamed in the light from the big bay window. Dee moved up beside her and stood quietly.

"This is a fine young woman, John. Darby told me where she lived, that you had known her. I brought you here in a cab. After they—When the police had—" She stopped, unable to continue.

I pulled on her hand. A strange foreboding seeped into the cheerful room, extinguished my straining heartiness.

"Darby. What happened to Darby? That's it, isn't it? The knife—I saw it go in. Maggie, he saved my life."

"Yes," she said simply.

"He fought, Maggie. Oh, how he fought. Like all the tigers in the world."

"Because he had something to fight for. That's all anyone needs."

I sat up. Maggie moved closer, her fine skin grey under the porcelain powder.

"They put Darby under arrest, Johnny. For murder."

I think I'd known it all along. Somehow.

I said, "Murder…" and the word tasted bad.

"Yes. That man, Eddie Samuels. He died. Darby beat him to death. He's in jail. Charged with homicide."

"Not first degree. They couldn't."

"Yes," Maggie said, impatient now. "They could and they have. You forget Darby was a licensed fighter. That makes any attack by him with his fists a deadly weapon charge. Whether or not they can prove murder is another thing."

"I see. And that means, to get him off, to show strong enough justification, we have to trot out—Johnny Babcock."

The name seemed to echo. It was the first time I'd said my own name in a long while. It felt strange, alien.

"In all his infamy," I said. "Johnny Babcock, the All-American chump!"

I looked out at the rooftops, square and bright in the sun. A bell tinkled from the street below as a Good Humor man worked the neighborhood. My jaws hurt from clenching.

"Johnny," Maggie said. "I don't know the whole story. Probably no one does, but you. Dee only told me that she had thought you dead. And then I got some old newspapers, found out about the insurance, your wife—about your supposedly burning up in a wreck."

"Go ahead, finish it. Say you drew the obvious conclusion."

Dee said, "Oh, Johnny, we're not accusing you of anything. All we want to do is help you."

I turned to her; her face was pale, full of concern. But I couldn't be sure. I couldn't ever be sure again. My face felt ice cold and stiff as a frozen hide. I said nothing.

"Johnny, please..."

"Just a minute." Maggie said. "What about Darby?"

I looked at them. The women in my life. A man never gets away from them. Sooner or later you've got to accept that.

"I want to tell you. Both of you. What I did, how it was." I got a cigarette from a pack on the table, busied myself lighting it. "Get a couple of chairs. This could take some time."

Maggie didn't move; her dark eyes never left my face. Dee brought a chair for the older woman, perched on the bed herself.

She was careful not to touch me. I sucked a long hot drag of the cigarette into tender lungs, let it out.

"Here it is," I said. "In order to get Darby off, I have to turn myself in, explain the ruckus in the bar. Why someone would want to kill me. When I do that, I die—in the gas chamber."

Dee closed her eyes, swayed a little. Maggie sat back in her chair; her face was composed except for tight lines around the eyes. And I told them. The whole story, neither embellishing nor leaving out.

No gloss, no whining. Just the straight story the way I'd lived it. And in the telling I purged myself a little of Edna. For she'd been with me always; through the wine stupors, the hurt of the beating. I began to lose Edna when I realized that the blame for what we'd done would never fit her shape alone, as I'd tried to convince myself. It wouldn't wash. The ultimate culpability was mine. With that knowledge came release from the crippling hiding and cringing, freedom from the bewildered fearing and wandering.

When I'd finished the story the sun had dropped low, squatting over the distant Pacific. The slants of the dying orb lanced upward over the sill of the bay window, diffused by blowing curtains, and mottled the walls and ceiling. For a long time the slow drip of a kitchen faucet was the only sound in the big, comfortable room.

I blew out my breath finally, breaking the spell. Dee stretched out toward me, her hand clutching my knee.

She said, "Johnny—was she ... very beautiful?"

Her face, without makeup, streaked with tears, was so different from the hard, wise, glamour mask it had been when I'd first seen her on that long ago night in the bar. I tried to smile for her, let her know I'd been wrong in not speaking, not acknowledging her aid. My lips were stiff.

Finally I just said, "Yes," not trying to bend it one way or the other. "Very beautiful. She still is."

Dee dropped her forehead to my leg, lay there. Her short fingers furrowed the sheets.

Maggie said, "You didn't kill the man, Johnny. I believe you. We'll make them believe you—somehow."

"It's not that easy. It doesn't make any difference. I made all of the preparations. I'm as guilty as if I had swung that tire iron myself."

"But you said—"

"I know what I said." I got another cigarette lit; lips twinging with the action. "I said Edna killed him while I was being sick like a baby, like a gutless fool, on the porch. And that's the way it happened. But makes no difference. Not to the law. Even if I could prove it."

"Then that's what you have to do," Dee said.

"Yeah, sure. I have to prove Edna tried to have me killed. Then use that for a—" I stopped. It might just be possible.

"What is it, John?"

"The other man. What happened to him?"

"He got away, John. The police got a description from me and from Darby. They're looking for him."

I sat up straighter. "Yeah, that could be it. That could be it."

Maggie stood up. "What about Darby?"

"Yes. What about Darby?" I pushed the half-smoked cigarette into the ashtray, leaned back. "This would be the spot to make the grand gesture. To say, all right fellas, take me in. No greater love, and all that. But I'm not going to do it. I'm not going to do it because that's what I've been doing for years—letting things happen to me. It's too god-damned easy."

"Johnny, listen..."

"No. You listen. I've sat back while an ambitious woman stole my identity and I've held my tongue. Because I was scared, too. But even more I didn't want to do anything to hurt Edna."

"What do you intend to do?"

"Make Edna confess. I don't know how, or how long it will take. But that's what I'm going to do."

"I brought the money," Maggie said. She pulled a folded bunch of bills from her coat pocket. "Do you…"

"Yes, I want it. And I'm going to use it. Give it to Dee."

The girl brought her head up from the coverlet. Her eyes were wet and clear as a sapphire sea.

"Whatever you decide, Johnny, include me."

Maggie said. "Johnny, you won't forget Darby?"

"I won't forget Darby. You tell him I'm going to get him out."

I turned back to Dee. In that moment it was suddenly as it had been in the bar that night—warm and comfortable, a deep communication.

I said, "What do you want, Dee? You've kept me here, got me attention. It's fair to ask your wishes."

She didn't hesitate. "I want you, Johnny. Any way at all. With patio and the time payments. Or running from the police, if that's what you decide to do. I want whatever you want. I'll do whatever you do."

"Dee…"

She slid off the bed and looked at Maggie, her eyes narrowing. The soft look was gone. "If that makes me a weak fool, well, that's the way it'll be."

Maggie just looked at her; the dark eyes brimmed. She nodded.

"All right," I said, as evenly as I could manage. "Let's get to cases."

"Do you think you can do it, John?"

"I don't know. But I'm going to try. I'm going to fight."

"We are," I agreed. "Maggie, I need three weeks. If the bed, took my hand.

"We are," Dee said and, walking to the other side of I can't do it in that time, I can't do it at all. Will you agree not to call the police on me for three weeks?"

"Of course." Her mouth quirked. "I wouldn't call them anyway. I'm too much a Fifth Streeter for that. But I can't let Darby suffer for an unjust thing. He killed that man to keep him from killing you, John. You go ahead, prove it. And remember your friends if you need help."

"I will, Maggie. I will."

She brushed quickly at her eyes, turned for the door. "Maggie..." I said. She stopped and turned, and I added, "Say hello for me, will you?"

She nodded and left quickly, almost running.

Dee walked slowly around the bed, her eyes never leaving my face. Tear streaks broke the smooth line of her face Her hips worked smoothly under the lime dress and she held her shoulders back, pushing out her fine, small breasts.

I said, "This bandage. We have to get it off my eye so that..."

She came close, just looked at me. Her lips opened and her tongue flicked them. A slow smile began.

"The uh, bandage," I said. "First we have to get some aric borid—some boric..."

"Shhh," she said.

"Solution. To wash the eyes. First, that..."

"First this," she said and kissed me. Soft, open lips touched mine, clung—but carefully, remembering my hurts.

I pulled her onto the bed with me. She was so light, so perfect.

I pulled my lips away, buried them in her summer-smelling hair. "I'm wounded," I whispered. "You'll kill me."

"Suffer," she said and found my lips again.

Matinee...

CHAPTER FOURTEEN

hateau Beauvais flattens one of the knobs on Sunset Boulevard where the section known as the Strip begins. A tall hedge—rough, thick stuff imported from England or somewhere—grew all along the Sunset side of the property. The taxi nosed through a narrow cut in this barrier and followed a short drive to the Chateau's front door. It was currently the place to go, and cars dotted the compact parking lot; attendants in long, red smocks and berets performed mechanical legerdemain with Austin-Healeys and Lincolns, Porsches and Cads.

It was a low building, expensively weathered, with curving shingles dripping from the roof and some architect's idea of French gingerbread in the fancy window style and patterned eaves. French Colonial. There was no neon, no marquee and no flashing lights.

"This is some joint," I said, when the cab had dropped us beside the iron-bound door. "You sure this is the place?"

Dee said, "This is the place. Don't be nervous. You look wonderful, darling."

"I bet."

I ran a hand over my face. The ridge where the chain had bit was still vivid; the cheekbone had healed, leaving a slight depression. Most of the minor cuts and bruises had gone away or mellowed, except for a few dark places under both eyes. I looked far from good. And I knew it.

Dee stood on tiptoe and straightened my tie. New, like the rest of the outfit. The suit was dark blue and fitted my slowly filling form to a comfortable exactness. Dee had done very well in choosing and buying for me.

"You look dangerous and continental." She kissed my nose with puckered lips. "Like a handsome, dashing Graham Greene character on his way to sweet-talk the beautiful but not very bright mistress of the commissar out of the secret plans."

I laughed. The door opened, spilling light. I took her arm.

"Come, Sascha…"

One of my precious three weeks had fled. The day after Maggie's visit to the Bunker Hill place I had begun in earnest to find the man named Weddo. The one connection to Edna and the attack on me—and a possible lever to use on her. The first thing I discovered was that the name was Huero—pronounced like it had two d's. Huero was a very common nickname among the considerable Mexican-American population of Los Angeles. That made it nice. Like hunting in New York for a guy called Smitty.

For three long, frustrating days I walked the hostile streets of East Los Angeles. Half the joints on Soto had seen my bandaged face and shambling walk. But it was useless. It was even a little bit funny. Whenever one of the Mexicans I questioned didn't want to talk—which was most of the time—I got the no comprendo bit. That's pretty tough to get around when you can't handle the language.

My health improved with each mouthful of the rich food Dee prepared for me. We didn't lack for personal interest. We were discovering each other, a process any young couple knows about. Everything was fine but the sex, and that was my fault. There seemed to be something—some tiny degree of rapport—absent in our relations. But time would take care of that, she was certain. I was hopeful.

Dee rented a small spinet and I played by the hour. The music was good for both of us. We made plans for my going on with music after the mess was cleaned up one way or the other.

So the days passed. And I got no closer to the man I had to find. My moods grew darker. Dee's vivacity increased correspondingly. She tried very hard. But I could see no end—no hope for a way out.

After a week of tramping aimlessly and futilely, I had returned this morning weighed down with physical fatigue and a keening frustration. The remodeled flat, usually a haven, oppressed me. I snapped at Dee. It was barely eleven and the day stretched out before me. I had exhausted all of my slim leads. I could not find Huero.

I took off my coat, threw it in the direction of the couch and strode to the window. From there I could see the sprawling roofs of lower Los Angeles, the rising rectangles of the business district. Dee came up behind me.

"No luck, darling?"

"None. Not a damn bit. I went to the agency like you suggested. He couldn't take the case without more to go on. And he didn't like my story."

"We'll find him, Johnny." Her arms went around me from behind; she rested her head between my shoulders. I was tense, unbending. "You wait, Johnny. By the time—"

"Wait!" I spun, shaking loose from her. "How long do you think I can wait? I have to get to this Huero, and from him to Edna. And it had better be a broad trail or I'm no better off than before."

I walked to the piano, raised the keyboard lid. Dee stayed by the window. She wore a quilted hostess gown and her hair was pushed up away from neck and ears. Her slim back was a straight line of disapproval.

She spoke without turning. "This is no good. Every day, searching, looking in the dark. All you know is the guy's nickname, and he wears a leather jacket. It's no good. We need help—professional help."

I plunked a key, sat down. "Yeah," I said. "Help. That's what I need. Old helpless Johnny. Get someone to the rescue quick, before he puts kerosene in the fire extinguisher."

"Johnny..."

The piano keys mocked me with their clean ivory exactness and I slammed both fists down in a furious discord.

Dee whirled from the window. "Stop it! Right now. Quit feeling sorry for yourself. All right, so you're not Sam Spade. I love you, Johnny. I want you with me from now on. More than I've ever wanted anything. If I have to make you mad at me to do it, then that's the way I'll play. So you listen..."

I grunted, not moving.

She turned toward the window, twisting her hands in the pockets of the gown. I straightened, watched her. "While you were gone this morning, I started thinking. I called a man I know who knows about such things. He tells me there are two ways to trace a man."

"You called—"

"Wait, Johnny. Two ways. One, you follow him from the point of whatever action you're investigating. Like you're trying to do. Right?"

I nodded. "Go ahead," I said tightly.

She came back, sat with me on the piano bench. "Two you backtrack on his life. Find out everything you can about him. Then go on from there."

"Oh, that's fine. But I have no connection. No hook to hang a line of search on. I don't know his name. The name he uses is as common as smog."

"You know Eddie Samuels' name."

I straightened. "What did you say?"

"Samuels. Don't you see, darling. If Samuels knew this Huero well enough to take him along, why there must be a connection in his past. Between the two. One must lead to the other—somewhere."

"Dee, you might have it." I jumped from the couch, grabbed her. "That might just do it."

And then it hit me. I had no real lead to Samuels. Except that he had tried to kill me and been killed in the process. I couldn't go ask the police and the newspapers had given it no ink to speak of. I pushed Dee away.

"What's the matter?"

I cursed under my breath. "If I just knew anything at all about this Samuels. Anything. Somewhere to start."

"Johnny..."

"An agency, I guess. I hate to, but it's the only way."

"Not the only way, Johnny." Dee followed me to the couch, sat beside me. She held her knees together, robe pulled tight. "You've never mentioned the way we met. And I appreciate it very much. You knew without my saying it that I hadn't—that I never went out again after the night in the bar."

"Dee, don't. There's no need. There really isn't."

"Listen." She took a breath. Her slightly tilted eyes were cast down and her blunt fingers plucked at the quilting of her housecoat. "Anyway, during the months I wo—What I mean is. I know a lot of people." Her eyes came up. There was a deep, flowing thing there—grey and somber.

"Men," she said. "All kinds of men. Mostly big wheels and semi-big wheels. Like Doctor Long. What I'm trying to say is the guy I called today will help us. Help you."

She waited. The silence came on, filling the space between us. I didn't move. My thoughts ran around and I wanted to hit something. All my vows. All my high-sounding protestations. Old Jungle Johnny.

All I could say was, "No." Cold, flat. I rubbed a hand carefully over the scabs, fingered the dent near the cheekbone. "No. This is my fight—my life."

"Johnny, listen. I know it's important to you that you do this yourself. More important than anything. But we can't just let everything go because you're out of your element and won't admit it."

"I'll find him."

"And Darby?" She moved against me, almost roughly, grasped my head between her hands. "He's waiting, Johnny. You can't let him down. And me ..."

Her lips touched mine, backed off just a fraction. "I can't lose you, darling. Don't be stubborn."

Here it was again. And here was Johnny Babcock again. I let her kiss me, soft and not insistent. My arms went around her.

Now, sitting in the low-lighted elegance of the Chateau Beauvais, all of my misgivings returned. Dee sat across from me at the small table. On my right a piano-bar was getting action from the dinner jacket set; a smooth young man with impossible teeth and a tinkling way with a ballad played between free drinks and frequent interchanges with the customers. The women seemed all pressed from the same mold—tall and lithe, and expertly made up and expensively gowned. The men looked bored. Small talk and bar sounds hovered, captured by the massive oak-beamed ceiling.

"Worried, darling?"

I turned to Dee. "Yeah. A little. This guy, this cop—can we trust him?"

She nodded, sipped her Martini. Her tilted eyes peered at me over the rim. She gave me a half smile and wrinkled her nose. "He'll be here. No law against having fun in the meantime. You're a heckuva fella. Haven't even asked me to dance. I'll burn the microfilm plans, that's what I'll do."

I started to answer but Dee forestalled me. She looked over my shoulder, said. "Here he is, Johnny. There's Rudy now."

Lieutenant Rudy Dembrun was a runt, but an effective and capable looking one. Dark and much too well dressed to be a cop, he was about thirty, wide in the shoulder and sure on his feet. A good suit was draped on his compact body and looked at home there. His eyes were dark-hued and his face kept its own counsel. I could see him ruining a squad room poker game.

After the introductions, the scrambling for an extra chair, we settled down. The waiter brought a drink and Dee exchanged the "what have you been doing?" type of dialogue with the short man for a moment. Then there was a brief silence.

"So you're Johnny." The dark eyes brushed me, seemed to see everything there was to see in that one, swift appraisal. "That's quite a weal there. Bicycle chain?"

I nodded, could say nothing.

"The one that got away," he said. "You know, Dee, you're stretching our friendship. This guy's wanted pretty good downtown. Here we got a wino charged with homicide and an eye witness does a fade." He shook his head, dipped quickly into his drink. "Good. Must use Johnny Walker on the bar. Anyway, Mr. uh—"

"Johnny. Just Johnny."

He shrugged. "Okay. You saw the thing in that joint?"

"Yes. And the man you're holding killed him, all right. But it was a justifiable killing. Believe me."

"Doesn't matter what I believe, fella. But a bunch of good cops're working real hard on that case. Some of 'em're looking for you. Why don't you come around and clear the thing up? It doesn't touch me, you understand. I'm bunco. But I'm a cop first. I don't like this at all."

Dee said, "Rudy..."

"Yeah, sure. I promised." He patted her hand. A quick, dark grin chased over his face. "This is a champion, Johnny. You know? One of the real good ones. You're lucky."

"Look, Lieutenant—".

"Rudy. We're friends here. If we weren't I'd be fitting you for stainless steel jewelry about now."

"Rudy," I conceded. "I want very much to come in. And that's what I'm going to do. But first I have to get some information.

Otherwise I'll never be able to prove what Darby did was justified. Do you see?"

"No. I don't. I see a guy in bad trouble. So bad he walks into a meeting with a cop knowing damn well it might wind him up in the sneezer for the big rap." He snapped a pack of cigarettes with his finger, selected one. "You must need that information real bad. Why don't you let us get it for you? It's our business, kid. We're pretty good at it."

"I can't. But I'll come to you the minute I can. That's a promise."

"Not me. Take it where it belongs. I could get transferred to Lincoln Heights for this if my boss found out. So don't forget to keep me out of it."

Dee sat stiffly, hands on her knees. She started to speak, stopped. Dembrun sat back in the chair. He clasped his fingers on the table and stared at the clutter of glasses and ashtrays on the white linen.

"Okay," he said. "I'll help. Shoot."

"Oh, Rudy, thank you so much," Dee said. Her hand clutched his arm.

"Sure, sure. You wanted to know about Eddie Samuels. Here it is. He was small time all the way. Made the whole route from snatching purses to armed robbery. That last got him a fast five upstate. He got out two years ago, hasn't been around since—in jail, that is. Born in L.A. Worked here and there around the town. Mostly in half-legal things—book runner, pool hustler—the whole bit. Fought a little ten years ago, but couldn't take a punch."

I leaned forward. "What about his—"

"You want to hear this, or not?"

"Yes. Certainly."

Dembrun pulled the chair closer to the table, finished his drink. "All right. Father and Mother dead. For the last couple years he's been minor muscle for a poker parlor in Gardena.

Floorman, they call 'em." He snorted, went on. "No known connections with the man being held, Darby Danbury. He—"

I said, "Please. Just Samuels. I know about Darb. There's no
connection. If you could tell me where Samuels lived, who he
associated with …"

"Okay. Here's the address. And a list of his known associates."

The piece of paper he brought forth sparkled in the artifi-
cial light. I wanted to reach out and snatch it, but I fought the
impulse.

I said, "Anybody on there named Huero? Or anything
like it?"

He looked, shook his head. "No." He held the paper away
from my reaching fingers, scowled at me. "Wait. What's the
Huero bit? That's a nickname, not a name."

"That chain." I gestured at my face. "He's the guy, this Huero.
Samuels and this guy tried to kill me. Darby stopped them. I've
got find the Mexican before I can take Darby off the hook. That's
it. Without this Huero I can't prove a thing."

"You might just want to get to this guy before we do for your
own reasons." The dark eyes drilled mine, turned to the girl.
"What do you think? This guy playing me for a sucker, honey?"

Dee's eyes flicked to me, then to Dembrun. They were wide,
steady. "No," she said quietly. "He's just tired of being one himself, Rudy. I'd bet my life on him."

"You would?"

She dropped her eyes and her hands got busy on her lap. So
low we had to lean forward to hear, she said, "Yes. As a matter of
fact, that's just what I have done."

Dembrun bobbed his head, kept it up. "Okay. Okay. Now, if
these don't pan out I can pull the whole package. It might take a
little doing but I can do it. Maybe you won't need it. Christ knows
you haven't told me anything. If you do need the rest, if these
leads come up blank, have Dee call."

"Thanks, Rudy. Thanks a lot. Someday you'll know how much you've done."

"Save it." He stood. "Way I see it, you're gonna root around in Samuel's past till you come up with Huero. That it?" I nodded and he continued, grinning. "Good, sound police procedure. And you might as well start right here."

"Here?" Dee asked.

"Here. Eddie had a brother. Charles. Sandy, he's called professionally. He might give you something. That's why I suggested this place when you called." Dembrun turned, jerked his sharp chin in the direction of the noisy piano-bar. "That's him playing. The one with the teeth."

He winked at Dee. nodded to me and walked away.

CHAPTER FIFTEEN

Dee wanted to wait until the club had cleared for the night to approach Sandy Samuels. But impatience was on me like a summer sweat. No sooner had Rudy Dembrun left the Chateau Beauvais than I maneuvered a seat at the thin coping surrounding the young man's piano, leaving Dee to fend for herself at our table. A waiter brought me a drink. I swished it idly, watching the pianist.

His long, white fingers walked confidently over the keys. He had a very facile technique, as mechanical as his smile. My sober contemplation attracted him finally. He turned his head, the smile increasing like sudden headlights around a curve.

"Like it?"

"Not much," I said. I pointed to my drink, asked a question with my eyebrows.

"No, thanks," he said, glancing for a moment at the keys, then back to me. "One of the hazards of the job. I try to limit my nightly intake."

I nodded, sipped my own drink cautiously. It hadn't been too long since my whole life had been one form of alcohol or another. Samuels ended the number with a clever run and a bent chord. There was a light patter of applause. He looked up at me, grinned widely.

"Sophisticated audience," he said, and swept into a bolero with a heavy, staggered beat.

I shook my head, allowed a small smile to touch my lips. Over the music, he said, "Why don't you like it?"

I shrugged. "Ricky-tick."

"One for you right now, then."

He stopped in mid-beat, shouted "Hey!" and picked up the beat with a solid thumping left hand and the bolero had become mambo, a frantic, pulsing thing in the modern idiom. He looked up at me briefly, hands leaping over the keys. I nodded and listened respectfully. Sandy Samuels could play a piano.

I forgot for a moment the grim purpose of my visit and just relaxed in the buttery flow of the music. It was liquid and lumpy and it swung like crazy. Even the hard-shell movie people, who made up most of the considerable crowd, quit whispering and false-laughing to listen. My fingers moved on the wood with the dancing notes. Abruptly, it ended. The writhing mambo notes had hardly drifted through the smoke to the beamed ceiling when a new sound came from the piano. This one you had to listen to—closely. It started low, almost formlessly, notes marching singly and standing alone in solemn order. Then silence. Nobody moved. Nobody said a word. Samuel sat, staring intently at the keys and he wasn't smiling. On silent cue he slithered curved hands up from his lap onto the waiting keys. He closed his eyes and touched them with authority. Blues for Audrey. It was different enough from Dave Brubeck's original recording to be interesting, and close enough to it to be full of the same swinging-somber mood. Even without a wailing alto.

For five full minutes he embellished and improvised— nothing but piano. Very close to being great piano. And there was no applause when he'd finished. But neither was there an immediate resurgence of the small talk and quick laughter. It took a while for the music to wear off. And this is perhaps the ultimate tribute for a performer. In the hiatus, Samuels and I went outside into the moon-silvered parking lot. The air was hot but clean and good.

"Smoke?" I held out the pack. Samuels turned, frowning. Then the smile came, slowly, not too deep. He took a butt, stuck it in the corner of his mouth. "What were you proving in there?" I asked.

I held a match and he sucked the cigarette alive, held the smoke.

He said, "I'm damned if I know. You said the secret word, I guess." White smoke billowed with the words.

"Sorry."

"No. Not at all. Once in a while I get sick of being a frozen smile and background music for seduction scenes."

I leaned against the rough side of the building. The soft night had taken good hold and the sky was black velvet. There were no stars.

We smoked. A car rushed through the hedge, rocked to an expensive stop at the door. I could just see the front of the place from my position. A tuxedo climbed languidly from the driver's side and aided a tall, wonderfully built, chestnut-haired woman to alight from the other. She wore a gown of electric blue so simple it must have cost more than the car. It hugged the lush body, shadows appearing where curves deepened. There were highlights in the dark hair; copper magic, flowing with changing light.

Samuels said something. His back was to the woman. I didn't hear. This was the first time I'd seen Edna for quite a while. She was beautiful—as always. I felt the powerful pull of her. Perhaps I'd never escape wanting her physically. No wonder she wanted everything in the world; with such beauty it must have been intolerable for her to be chained to one man, one life.

"You listening?"

"Humh? Oh, yeah." I turned away from my memories, sternly told myself to get to the point with this young man and be on my way. "You said Tristano was the only true teacher since Hartvig. I agree. But with people like Pfieffer and Powell and Monk the experimentation goes on. I think—"

Samuels said, "What are we talking about?" He grinned. "I'm not going to give up this easy buck. And we both know it. I just felt like cutting loose there for a moment. Don't expect any more of it."

"I don't understand. The people liked it. Why not play it all the time?"

"Sure they did. It's good music. But you don't drink when you listen to jazz." He flipped the cigarette and it spiraled out over the hedge, disappeared. "Surveys. Best music for drinking is 'undistinguished.' And that's a quote."

Samuels glanced at his watch. "Gotta go. I got to finish a long set. Got a date tonight with the most beautiful woman in the world. I'll introduce you."

"Look, Samuels..."

"I got to go, man." His teeth flashed. "The libido calls. I am but a humble male."

"Wait. I want to see you. Take a minute, no more."

"You sound serious."

"I am. I want to ask you a couple of questions about your brother."

"My—" His lips tightened and a line appeared between his eyes. He was small but the way his shoulders stiffened, I could tell he was ready for anything. "Eddie. Poor Eddie. What could anyone want with him now? You a cop?"

"No. I'm just a—Well, look. If you'll tell me a few things I'll get out of your face, and you won't have to think about it."

"It's a distasteful subject." He walked to the hedge on the canyon side, looked out. "Eddie and I were never close. I was the lucky one. He was the one everybody beat on. What do you want to know? And why do you want to know it?"

"You saw the scar on my face, the marks?"

"Yes. Did Eddie do that?"

"Some of it. He and another man. A Mexican called Huero. That's what I want from you. Any connection at all to this Huero."

"Wait a minute. You the guy they were beating up on when that punchy killed him? Well, now, what do you know about that."

We stood there in the murky light of the Chateau Beauvais' parking lot and eyed each other like two suitors for the same girl. His eyes had narrowed, become completely secretive. I felt the change. Somewhere I'd said the wrong thing.

I said, "Look. The guy that killed your brother did it to save my life. That's the way it is. I'm sorry if it hurts you to think of your brother that way. But there's another life involved now. Darby—that's the fighter—"

"I know. Darby Danbury."

"Yes. The reason they were beating me is of no interest to you. But I have to find Huero in order to prove that what Darby did was justified."

"What was the reason? I'm interested. I'm real interested."

"What for? It's nothing to you."

"Eddie's something to me. You want to make him out a murderer. Drag the name in the mud some more."

"But that's what he was doing! Trying to kill me."

"That's what you say." Samuels lit a cigarette quickly, tilting his head to escape the heat of the match. "I say if you want information, go to the cops. I already talked to them."

"All I want—"

"I know what you want and I'm not telling you anything."

"Look, Samuels—"

"No looks. No nothing," he said and took off, weaving his way through the array of expensive automobiles.

DEE HADN'T MOVED. The pile of butts in the ashtray testified to the length of my absence. And the shine of her eyes said something about six or seven Martinis. As I approached, she tugged at the dipping neckline of her saffron gown and looked at me frowningly. Her pouting lips were red and wet.

"Do any good?"

I shook my head, took out money for the check. She looked at my face and wisely refrained from comment. She could see it had gone badly. As we prepared to leave, my eyes sorted the figures in the large room, looking for Edna. I couldn't find her. She certainly hadn't gone already. Dee folded her light stole over an arm. I picked up the change from the waiter's tray, left a tip and started for the foyer, Dee on my arm.

Halfway there, she said, "Johnny. Look at that woman."

"Which one?" I guided Dee along the lane next to the short bar, avoiding a laden waiter.

"Over there. See?" We stopped, pushed close to the bar so as not to obstruct the narrow walk-way between tables and bar. "The table just behind the piano. Right behind your friend. You can't see it if you don't know it's there."

It was Edna, of course.

"Isn't she beautiful?"

"In a way, I guess."

"In a way? She's a goddess." Dee gazed with unrestrained admiration at Edna. I watched her while she watched Edna. Dee's ripe lips opened and she sighed, fine rounded breasts outthrust in the tiptoe pose of peering. "Such hair. Oh, Johnny, if I looked like that I'd be so happy."

"I'm happy with you just the way you are."

Her head flashed around. The tilted eyes grew grave and she walked to me, dropped her forehead to my chest. We stood like that for just a moment. People around us chuckled. Dee looked up, eyes moist.

"The hell with you, guy," she said.

I smiled down at her and it was easy to do. "Now, Sascha, about those plans..."

She smiled. "Okay, Doc. Let's go see the etchings."

We started out. Passing the piano, my eyes drifted to the table behind. I couldn't do it. No way. I couldn't leave without seeing her. I turned without explanation and made my way through the midnight crush to the table. Dee followed in my wake, Edna, slim throat throbbing with polite laughter, was being the animated doll for the man sitting with her. The piano tinkled accompaniment.

I said, "Hello, Edna. Nice seeing you," and it came out deep and easy, without sticking at all.

Edna turned, still laughing. For a second she didn't recognize me. Then knowledge came, washing over her perfect face like an airplane shadow on a sunny field. Her hand went to her throat, and for an instant I thought she would scream. Not Edna. Not ever Edna. Her gray eyes narrowed and the hungry lips came together. She turned one way, then the other. The languid man just sat, a polite expression on his slightly vacuous features. Dee moved beside me. took my arm.

Edna said, "Johnny. This is a surprise."

She had recovered nicely. One hand reached for a thin-stemmed Martini glass, lifted it steadily. Her gaze slanted up at me.

"I imagine," I said.

"You seem to be doing better than you were when I last saw you."

Her eyes swept slowly over Dee, woman-appraising. A look of grudging approval touched her lips. She smiled.

"Indeed, better. A new secret, Johnny?"

"It's the scar. It adds a certain dash the women go for." I pulled Dee close to me. Her neat features were composed, social-stiff. "A little dash, you know?" I said.

She knew. Her fingers patted on the table and a trace of the high color I knew so well stained her face.

"You must tell me about it sometime. I really have been wanting to talk to you, Johnny. The day in the car, in that awful street..." She glanced at Dee, warned me with her eyes.

"Pretty dirty, wasn't it? That's my home, Edna. Has been for quite a while. You should try it. Put you in touch with your own mortality."

"You've changed, Johnny. There's a hardness, a cold core—something I've never seen in you. It makes you quite interesting. You always were handsome. And the scar does help. How did it happen?"

I almost hit her. But I laughed instead. "I owe it all to you."

She looked away quickly, said to Dee, "Is he really as virile as he looks, dear?"

She was trying to shock Dee. To divert me. She regretted it. Dee, standing with both hands clutching my bicep, looked at her blankly for a moment. Then she sucked in her cheeks and winked, broadly and obviously. Edna flushed. She reached for her glass, spilled it. When her eyes came up, fury leaped from the dark orbs. Shoulders hunched and breasts swelled, pushing a creamy line past the edge of her bodice.

"Get out of here!" she hissed. "Take your tramp and get out!"

I grinned. "Why, you're vicious, Edna. How could I ever have missed that? You're a vicious bitch!"

Her companion started. "Now, see here, old boy." He rose quickly. "Enough is enough. I can't sit here while you take—"

I got a fold of silk lapel and jerked the guy half over the table. The smile on my lips was stiff and probably very ugly. It felt that way.

"You sit. All right? You sit or I'll break your jaw."

I let go and he sat. Edna was speechless. And Dee made little silent motions of cheering and applause.

I said, leaning far over the table toward Edna, "You remember, sweetheart. I'm a very devious guy."

Dee and I got out of there. Edna called but we didn't stop. Strangely I wanted to laugh. Reaction, probably.

Waiting for a cab, Dee pressed close to me, looked long into my eyes. She nodded, kissed me quickly.

"Just one thing, Superman. She'll try again now, you know. Did you have to invite her to kill you?"

"I had to. I hope she tries."

A car honked. We ignored it. Her fingers rose to my face, traced the scar, lightly touched the dent under my eye.

"Dash," she said and we both laughed.

But still no Huero. I didn't stop to analyze why the piano player had been so friendly and then suddenly so rigidly hostile. Perhaps his feeling for a hoodlum brother was deeper than the impression he tried to give. At any rate, I had to write him off, start elsewhere in the tangled, dirty yarn that was the life of Eddie Samuels.

Rudy Dembrun had said Gardena. The Poker City, south of L.A. on Vermont, is just beginning to roll about midnight. We went directly there from the Chateau Beauvais. The cop hadn't said which of the town's five palaces of chance had employed Samuels. So we went from one to the other. The first two were blanks. A parking lot attendant in one had known Eddie, but not where he worked—or so he said. It was difficult to get information. Soto street and East L.A. all over again.

Back in the cab again, I dropped my head into my hands, rubbed my eyes. Dee's hand massaged my neck.

"Tired, darling?"

"Yeah."

"Discouraged?"

"No." I straightened. "What time is it?"

She looked. "One-thirty. Little more. They stay open till four. I asked the floorman at the last place."

I leaned forward, tapped the driver's shoulder. He turned his head slightly, keeping an eye on the rushing highway. "Stop just this side of the Domino. There's a bar next door. You go in there and have a couple of drinks. I'll come get you when we're ready to go."

He nodded and I handed him a bill.

"Is this it, Johnny? It's time we had a little luck."

"I hope so, Dee. I hope so. I want to get my life straightened out. Now, more than ever."

She murmured in her throat and fell against me, the stole slipping off of bare shoulders. She spoke softly against my cheek.

"Straight or crooked, it's our life—not yours."

CHAPTER SIXTEEN

Dee and I walked up the black-concrete walk of the Club Domino. It was quite a joint. The curving front wall was tinted glass. On each side of the main door, vertical louvres of black-stained redwood reached upward to a flat roof. Huge block letters of stark white spelled Domino Club across the face of the fluted front. Glass doors opened automatically as we broke a beam. On the doors, silhouette masks with hanging strings carried out the Domino theme. The reception room was black and white tile with a waterfall in one corner and luxurious modern couches spaced about.

Another set of double doors faced it. I pushed through, Dee right behind me. A uniformed man with a pistol in a hip holster stood just inside. He smiled at us, indicated the vast game room at his right.

"Wow," Dee said. "Reno on Saturday."

"Yeah. They do it up brown, all right. But just poker. Draw and lowball. Not stud."

The playing area was repressed from floor level. At least a hundred green-topped tables were surrounded by earnest gamblers. More than half of the players were women. Cute chip girls, wearing red bolero jackets and the tightest slacks imaginable, hurried here and there collecting the table rentals. They smiled and switched, making change and serving food and drinks right to the tables. All were young, all extremely pretty. I remembered one of them telling me once that hustling chips in Gardena was the only profession more lucrative to a smart girl than hustling her body.

A slightly amplified voice came over the several speakers. "J.D., two and four low. J.D., two and four low." A fat woman held up her hand, waddled over to the call-board and the floorman drew a line through her initials on the black surface. Another floorman, red jacket standing out among the players on the floor, shouted, "'Starting a four and eight low. Four players for a four and eight low. Table Twenty-three."

Dee nudged me. "Big business."

"It is. But our business is finding out if Eddie Samuels worked here."

We started walking, circling the playing area, toward the callboard. We moved slowly, watching the swirl and color, listening to the gambler-drone, the clack of chips.

"This is nicer than the others."

"There's another further down as nice as this. Maybe nicer. Let's go see that boardman. If Eddie worked the floor here, that guy would know."

The man at the blackboard smiled at our approach. He waved at the board.

"Pretty full right now," he said, "except for the new four and eight game. Draw or low tonight?"

"Low," I said. "Four and eight's a little rough for me. I might sit in and leave a call for a two and four opening. Okay?"

"Fine." His eyes went over Dee. Very slowly, as the dress and her good body deserved. He was frank about it, and Dee smiled prettily for him. "And you, miss—would you care to play?"

"No, I think not. I'll root for my man."

"Wouldn't have it any other way." the man said and picked up the small microphone hooked to the edge of the board. "Mike," he whispered into it. "Mike—a four and eight."

"By the way," I said, "I haven't been around for a while and I don't see Eddie tonight. He around?"

"Eddie? Eddie who, friend?"

The man turned, his face blank. His eyes moved around over my head.

"I never did know his last name. We went out to the beach a couple of times together. Good poker player. Big guy, kind of rough-looking."

"I wouldn't know."

I said, "Oh, now look. All I want to know is he around. That's all."

"Look, chum-boy," the little man said. "You got questions, ask 'em somewhere else. I got a room to run here."

His eyes looked like two nickels on a slab of wood. They blinked, held mine steadily. Suddenly the man didn't like me. And just as suddenly I saw that I'd been using the wrong approach all along.

The boardman said, "I'm scratching you, friend. You want to play, you go somewheres else."

I swung away without further word and made for the office. Should have done that to begin with. It was a door next to the cashier's cage, neatly lettered Manager. As I reached for the knob, a voice stopped me.

"You're just an action man, aren't you, Johnny?"

I turned. Sandy Samuels leaned against the rich wood paneling near the cage, flipping a stack of yellow chips in one long-fingered hand.

"Sandy." I noticed his cheeks were tight; he looked like a man nerving himself up to something. "Early for you, isn't it?"

He caught his chips in a fist with a snap, stepped forward. I looked down at him slightly. My back tensed and the muscles in my thighs bunched.

"You feel lucky, Johnny?"

"I don't know what you mean. Look, Samuels, you're beginning to bore me. Suppose you—"

"Bored is what you're likely to get, big man. You'd better listen to a guy that has your best interests at heart."

"That would be you."

"That would be me." He slid closer, narrowed his eyes. "You forget about my brother and what happened to him. Hear? Don't stick your fat beak in any further. This is a warning. A little more action from you and you're paid for."

I put four fingers and a thumb lightly on his chest. The light in the room had taken on a red tinge. I could feel blood in my face and I knew the scar must stand out like the Burma Road in moonlight.

"Go, musician." My throat was tight. "Go, before I—"

Samuels' eyes blazed and he whipped a bony fist at my face. Before it got close I shot-putted with the hand on his chest, catching his chin with the spread juncture of thumb and fingers. He sailed over the railing and landed in the middle of a table. The table buckled and chips flew, glasses broke. After the crash there was a hushed moment. I looked around—no way to get out, at least not safely. Dee was nowhere in sight and I was thankful for that. A man rushed up on my right. The little man from the board. I kicked him in the stomach and he collapsed.

"Pete!" someone yelled and the cop broke around the carpeted perimeter at me.

I vaulted the rail, landed among milling poker players and bending chip retrievers. Sandy Samuels was straightening and I pulled on his tie as he came around, slammed a right hand into his pretty face with all the spleen and fury built up by the past hours behind it. He fell like a toppled tree. My knuckles stung and I felt good as hell. I shouted for the hell of it and reached for a man in a red jacket.

Then the Chrysler building fell on me. I went down in sections, or it seemed that way. Blows hit and I sagged; more hits and I sagged some more. I felt the carpet on my face and then I gave up.

I was in a car. For a few fuzzy seconds I had no idea where I was or what the situation was. Then I became aware of a soft thigh under my cheek, solicitous hands on my head. I moved.

"Johnny. Johnny, are you all right?"

"I'm all right. Every time I get in a fight some woman has to rescue me. I'm fine."

"You did fine, Johnny. You should see that club."

I tried to sit up and the car swerved violently. I made it finally, looked out the window. Dark scenery flashed by. We were in the taxi, our taxi. Tearing along a narrow road with fields on one side and industrial buildings on the other. I could see no other traffic.

"Where are we?"

Dee turned from the back window.

"We were followed when we left the club. Joe said he could lose the tail this way."

"Joe?"

"The driver," she said. Then her hands patted at my face with a wispy handkerchief. "You're always getting belted. Can't you duck?"

I grinned in the darkness, a little ruefully. Dee's face was twisted oddly.

I said, "Where were you when I needed you, woman?"

"What do you think I am, a gun moll?" But her voice was shaky. She put her head down, blew her nose. "Now. Tell me. Why'd you hit that man? I didn't get to see anything. I was out in the parking lot. I just got there at the end."

"I don't know. It's funny. That Samuels had no more reason to lean on me than—than Joe, there. But he did. Heavy, too. Told me to forget his brother, keep my nose out of the whole thing if I valued my health."

"But why?"

"Beats me." I felt the back of my head with tender fingers. A lump. Getting used to those. No skin break; no mushy feeling of concussion. "There's something real odd there. Damn it, if I could only find that Mexican!"

Dee was trying to strike a match and the jouncing of the taxi kept her from succeeding. I took the matchbook from her.

"Light one for me."

I got the match lit, held it under the cigarette in her lips. She puffed once, then looked up and said, "I found him, Johnny. Huero."

I dropped the match.

"What did you say?"

"Johnny, the match. It's—"

I took her arms. "The hell with the match. Why didn't you tell me?"

"I'm sorry I didn't tell you right away. But it was such a hassle getting you out of there and everything."

"Tell me now. Tell me damn quick."

"I went out to talk to the parking lot attendant. You were headed for the office. I simply asked him if he knew Eddie Samuels. He didn't want to say anything at first. But I worked on him a little."

"Yeah." I lit another match, fired two smokes; hers had gone out. "Here," I said.

"Jealous, Johnny?"

"Dee. No games, huh? Not now. You know how important it is that I find this monkey."

"All right." She took a drag of her cigarette, the glow reddening her features. "The attendant said that he had an assistant who could answer anything I wanted to know about Eddie. They were buddies, he said, ran around together."

"Did you talk to the guy?"

"No. He wasn't there. Hasn't been to work for a week."

At that moment the cab turned off of the back road onto what looked like an upper Hollywood arterial. I didn't recognize it. I asked Joe.

"Wilshire," he said, throwing it over his shoulder. "About fifteen thousand. Where'll I go?"

"Just a minute. Dee, what the assistant's name? And did you get his address?"

She nodded, moved closer to me. "I got his address. A place called El Encanto on Orme street in East L.A."

"Where's that?"

"I don't know. But listen, Johnny. The assistant's name is Robert Vellardo. They call him Huero."

I heard it and sat back. The twinkling traffic on Wilshire came into focus; the lush night crept into the cab. For the first time since the fight at the Doniker I drew a complete breath. Huero. And Edna. Now I could dig. Now I could lean. Then—

"Joe wants to know where to go, Johnny."

"What time is it?"

I looked at my own wrist but there was no watch there, of course. Mine had ridden the death car into Angeles Canyon on the arm of George Carter.

"Just after three," Dee answered. "Johnny, let's go home. Your head is hurt and you're all messed up. Tomorrow you can start after Huero."

I brushed at the suitcoat. Just a little dust. One small tear at the shoulder. And a little blood from where a scab had been ripped off. It didn't matter.

"Bunker Hill, Joe."

The cab prowled the subsiding streets toward downtown Los Angeles. Dee smoked in silence and watched me. Her shoulders were bare.

"Hey. Where's your wrap?"

"I lost it. It doesn't matter. When the cop came…"

"Tell me. How did you get me out of there? Why didn't they arrest me?"

She turned on the seat, slid her legs up between us. Her face was a light blotch in the cab's gloom. "The policeman," she said. "Without him, we'd have been dead. I told him you were my lover and if the fight got into the papers your wife would have a fit."

"I'll be damned. And he went for it?"

She shrugged, grinned a little. "He had to. No one else knew the reason for the fight. Samuels, that pretty piano player, hadn't come to yet."

I grunted. Samuels puzzled me. Why should he care if I asked questions about his hoodlum brother? Certainly he wouldn't have any silly ideas about protecting the family honor or any of that jazz. But you never know.

The cigarette burned my fingers. I dropped it, stomped around on the floor mat, putting it out. The cab rolled down the depression where Wilshire dips between the two lakes at Westlake park. Dark, oily water, black as the surface of a trick mirror, shone at either hand. Reflections of late neon, slashing in color, from the bars and restaurants lining Alvarado, mottled the slick black. I leaned my head on the hard sill, let the warm air, cooling now in the hours toward morning, blow through my hair.

I DUMPED HER at the apartment on Bunker Hill. We had a fight about it but when the taxi roared away I sat in the back seat alone.

The Doniker was dark, long past closing. I left Joe in the cab, warning him about the hubcaps, and walked around to the rear through Nightmare Alley. It was the first time I'd been there in some time. The smell was oppressive. A month ago I'd become as accustomed to it as the odor of burning oil on the Freeway. Now it sickened me. Once I stumbled over a human obstacle. He didn't even grunt.

I banged heavily on the door, finally got Maggie out of her chaste bed. The fleeting thought came to me that if the wandering Halloran ever did come in the door, Mag would have to find a bigger bed to hold them both. A light went on inside. The door cracked open on night-chain and Maggie peered out, eyes swollen and cheeks puffed with sleep.

"Who is it? Who's out there?"

"About Ben Adam," I said. "Leading all the rest."

"Johnny!" She flipped the chain, threw wide the door. "Come in. Hurry. You shouldn't be around here."

I stepped inside. "I had to, Maggie."

"You look fine," the little woman said, "just fine. Here. Sit down while I—"

"This is business, Maggie." She wore a faded cotton robe over a long white nightgown. A frilled cap covered her head. "I got a lead on the guy who was with Samuels when he—when Darby killed him."

She clucked. "That Darby. He won't say a word to the police. When they ask your name he pulls that punchy act of his. Won't say a word."

I sat on the edge of the rocker. Maggie bustled at the stove, making coffee. There was no way I could get away from that, I knew.

"Have you seen him, Maggie? How is he?"

"I see him twice a week. All they'll let me." She bent, pushed a match under the iron kettle. A puff of flame washed out, then settled to a low burn. "He asks about you all the time. Says to tell you he'll wait until you get him out. He's a good boy, John."

"I know it." I got up suddenly and walked to the end of the room and back. "I shouldn't be here. But I need some help. Here's the bit. I've got—"

"Coffee, John? Be ready in a minute."

"Humh? Oh, no." I stalked to the chair, dropped on it. "Maggie, you told me I had friends. Well, I need 'em now. And I'm not so smart about it as I was, either."

"Don't worry about it, Johnny." She sat on the edge of the rumpled cot, pulled the robe over her legs. The tips of fuzzy, pink mules poked, somehow incongruously, from under the blue-stitched hem of the nightgown. "You were hurt."

"Here's how it is …" And I began.

❧   ❧   ❧

Twenty minutes later I sat at the small deal table in Maggie's room, talking with a wino named Murray Altrock. The lights had been turned off; only the gaslight from the one burner of the stove lit the room. Murray Altrock, a small man whose uncontrollable yen for tall women had ridden him to Fifth Street, had a peculiar hustle. He worked the east side of L.A.—Mexican territory. And did well at it. He was small and inoffensive, and perhaps he contributed to the morale of the Angelenos just by being a white man—and begging. At any rate, he knew the section. The people trusted him. Or maybe ignored him. I told him what I knew, the man I wanted to find.

"You sure picked a dilly, Johnny. A real dilly, now." He blinked, sucked at the coffee. We'd had to load him with coffee to shake him from the wine slumber Maggie had found him in. "Yes, sir. I know that place. El Encanto. Not on Orme, though. Fresno, maybe."

"Can you spot him for me? Just that. I'll get him."

"I'll try, Johnny." The little eyes squeezed together as Murray struggled to stay awake. "Give me a little money. Not much. Enough so's I can drink in the Encanto all day. Then I'll see you here tomorrow—today, I guess it is, now. Anyway, I'll be here. Give you the dope."

"Thanks a lot, Murray. It means a lot. Maybe my life."

"And maybe Darby's," Maggie put in quietly. She shuffled up to the table. "You be real careful, Murray Altrock. You hear? Don't get too drunk before you find out what John wants to know. Or you'll have no credit here again."

"Oh, I'll do it all right, Maggie. I like Johnny. Gee, that night you played the piano, Johnny. The guys still talk about it. How come you don't drop in?"

"Murray, listen. Don't forget to find out how I can get Huero out of there. He hasn't been to work since the fracas. I checked. So he's laying low with his own people. He may be hard to dislodge." I got up, walked to the now-open door leading to the main room.

The ugly old bar was a darker shape in the dark room. My eyes held one corner for a moment. There. Right there by the Dutch door.

Murray's voice brought me back. I suddenly realized how long the day had been. I was tired. Real, bone-deep, tired. And my head hurt.

"What, Murray?"

"I said, I'll find out for you. I'll find the guy. But you'll never just up and take him out of there. No way."

"But why?" I walked to him, looked down.

"That's in Whitefence," the little man said. "That's the toughest, knife-wieldingest hollow you ever seen. Whitefence is rough." His eyes flitted to the bills I held out; he took them. "I'll find out. But you'll get killed if you try to take him out of there. They hate gavachos. And they protect their own people, Johnny. They stick together."

"I'll get him," I said. And I believed it. I didn't know how; only that I had to do it. "I'll see you here."

"At four," Maggie put in. "That'll give you time to move tomorrow."

"Maybe," Murray said, rising. "Boy, that Whitefence is rough...."

He left, still murmuring. Maggie went back to bed, only minutes away from time to open the Doniker. I paid off Joe the taxi driver, thanked him, and took the Angel's Flight to Bunker Hill. And Dee.

CHAPTER SEVENTEEN

The lights were out in the converted brownstone. I opened the door, trotted silently upstairs. It was early-morning quiet and the secret sounds of a house in slumber came to me. I opened the door, stepped inside. The light flashed on as I did so. Dee was sitting curled in the big chair which she'd dragged over in front of the door. Her hand came away from the lamp's switch, her eyes dark and full of the question they'd been asking for weeks. Her lips put words to it.

"Now, Johnny?" The breathless voice pulsed at me. "Is this the time?"

The door swung shut behind me. I loosened my tie, pulled off the soaked coat, my eyes never leaving the tilted ones of the girl in the chair. Lamplight streaming, beauty soft and gently packaged, coming more to focus as the hard block of unclassifiable resentment inside me crumbled.

"Dee. Dee, my darling…"

Her eyes closed and the chair caught her head as she flung it back. Shadows swam in the hollows where the slanted light could not reach.

She whispered, "I knew, Johnny. I knew there in the Chateau. She won't be between us now."

Dee leaned hard against the back of the chair, stretched her legs full length. Quilted material fell away as she lifted them, straight and tanned and slim. One slipper fell off. She held out her arms, still not opening her eyes.

"Johnny…"

I scooped her up and her legs flopped over my arm, her arms went round my neck. She pulled my head down and opened tinted lips, body lifting to me.

This was the time.

Dawn came, red and grimy, before sleep claimed either of us. In the lush exhaustion I had told her of my plan and of her part in it. I didn't mention what Murray Altrock had said about getting Huero out of Whitefence. No need to worry her.

"One thing, Dee."

She murmured sleepily, rubbing her cheek on my arm.

"Dee..."

"Yes, darling. I'm listening. I love you."

"No. I want you to hear this. It's important." I pulled away, let her head fall on the crumpled pillow. "Even if it works, if Freese goes along—still I've got to go to jail. You know that?"

"I know it, Johnny." She shook her hair, got up on one elbow. "I'll be here, darling. Right here."

"Yes. We'll talk about that later. Right now I want to make sure you know what to do."

She sighed, lay back. "I'll get the insurance man up here. That's easy. Then it's up to you."

"I may be late. I don't know what I'll run into down there. But I'll get here. And I'll have Huero. What happens then depends on Mr. Albert Freese."

"You'll do it, darling. And we'll be the happiest couple in Sunny Dell Acres."

We kissed and it got tender and hot again. Light crept into the room from the sun and struck our bodies.

I said, "Dee. How about kids? Will we ..."

"Oh, yes, Johnny. Yours and mine." Her tone got fierce. "I'll be so good to them."

"Four," I said. "All boys. Right?"

"I don't care, I don't care!" After a long moment, she whispered, "One girl, Johnny? Just one..."

Maggie let me in the back door. She held a finger to her lips, motioned me to the corner. She jerked a thumb at the door to the bar, reached out and clutched air with her hand. Nabs in the Doniker. I asked if I should leave and she shook her head, went back into the main room.

I sat on the cot and closed my eyes. I'd awakened to an empty apartment. Dee had gone, leaving juice and coffee for me, a note covered with scrawled words and lipstick. She would spend the day shopping and getting what she termed "the works" at the beauty shop. Then she would make an appointment with Freese.

I had dressed carefully—nylon zip jacket, light slacks, rubber-soled shoes and a dark shirt. Then I went to a barber shop for a shave. After that, with hours to kill, I'd walked up to the towering, grey mass of the Hall of Justice.

I saw a bus. It was a Flexible, new and glinting in the afternoon sun. The windows were barred. Behind the policeman driver, a heavy screen ran from floor to ceiling, separating a motley assortment of prisoners from two additional guards in the driver's compartment.

The bus passed me slowly. Faces hung out the windows— wise, faded, dirty, hopeless, handsome—all kinds of faces. Some sucked on cigarettes. Others sat quietly, eyes darting to the swing of women's hips in the city street, the flashing neon of a bar. Like squirrels storing nuts, they gathered impressions against the long, hungry time. The bus limped over the rise at the parking gate, turned laboriously down the hill toward Spring Street. The faces looked. I just stood.

I walked away from there and thought about the faceless faces sucking sunlight through barred windows. And about Darby.

I thought about them, now, on the cot in Maggie's room waiting for the little wino to bring me news from Whitefence. There were many images; all messed up with Darby and myself and Dee and Edna.

Maggie opened the door, letting in a murmur of sound from the main room. She stepped through.

"Murray's here," she said. Her hands, white and puckered from washing glasses, fussed with the immaculate pink sweatshirt. "I'll bring him in. But you be quiet."

"What time is it?"

"Still not three. About quarter to. He's early." She reached for the knob. There's a cop out there. Been all morning."

"Stake-out?"

She nodded. "All dressed up. Dirty jacket, beard—the whole thing." Maggie's powder-white face twisted in a quick grin. "He just doesn't make it. Nobody's spoken to him yet. He can't understand it."

The Brotherhood is sensitive. There's a look in a man's eyes when he has accepted the oath, thrown away pretense and assumed a readiness for complete degradation. No cop could fake it.

Murray Altrock weaved through the door, closing it carefully behind him. His little red eyes burned cheerfully. He was drunk, of course. But not enough to impair his ordinary abilities.

"Fuzz out there," he said.

"I know. Sit down." I drew a chair to the table, indicated the rocker for him. "What about Huero?"

"I saw him. Skinny kid, twenty-something. Got a sneery way of looking at you. Crazy laugh. That him?"

"Yes. Where, Murray?"

"Where you said. El Encanto." His small features lit. "Had a doll with him, a Mexican chick. Tall, fine—stood about five-eleven. Bigger'n him. Boy, was she stacked."

"Murray, never mind the tall broad. What I want is Huero." I ripped the top off a cigarette pack, tore a couple loose. "Here. Tell me about Huero."

"Sure. Sure, Johnny." Murray took the butt, played with it in dirty fingers. "But this broad. Was she—" He saw my eyes, switched suddenly. "It's in Whitefence. Like you said. And the street ain't Orme. It's the next one down, toward Fourth. Toward the section they call Tortilla Flats."

Murray's eyes blinked. He rubbed his four-day beard. Then he pulled a piece of paper out of his pocket, smoothed it on the table. It was a comprehensive, house by house map of the area. Quickly, wasting no words, he sketched the place verbally. As he talked, I began to see what he meant by Whitefence being rough.

A hollow, it lies below the level of Whittier Boulevard, past Boyle Heights in that area known to natives as Tortilla Flats. One street leads down to it from Whittier; a dead-end named Bernal, or something similar. There was one other means of egress, Fresno Street, which dead-ends a block over from Bernal. Fresno skirts the Flats proper.

"All Mexicans?"

"All." Murray hunched over his crude map, pushed a grimy nail on the paper. "See here? That's a dirt road you might be able to use getting out. But don't try it till you go over it at least once. It's tricky. You gotta have a car. There's no street action, no traffic to speak of. No cover. I don't think you can do it. Why don't you put the cops on him? They can drag him out."

"I can't. Look, the Encanto is where?"

"Right here. The next street down from Orme. I don't know the name. Maybe it ain't got one. No signs. I looked." He looked up. "A reggela Dick Tracy, huh?"

"Is there anything else I should know before I creep into the lion's den?"

"Just be careful, Johnny. Real careful. Them Mexicans stick together something fierce. And they'll hurt you. Especially trying to kidnap one of their boys. And you'll stick out like an albino in Harlem, so you'll have to get in and get right out."

"I intend to."

"One more thing." The little man leaned forward, rolling his cigarette between his palms. "All the other Mexicans hate Whitefencers. The ones from Whittier and Boyle Heights, Soto and Bellflower. They hate 'em because they're rat-packers. So when you go into White-fence a stranger, you're in trouble even if you're a Mexican. You see?"

"No. But that's all right. What's a rat-packer?"

"Oh, you know—a bunch on one. Like a pack of rats. Well, that's the way they fight around Whitefence. So nobody likes 'em. But nobody messes with 'em in their home territory. You just be careful."

"I hope he's there when I hit, that's all."

"Huero? He'll be there, all right. That girl of his, the tall one. She's—"

"All right, Murray."

"No, listen." His red-rimmed eyes were hurt. "She lives there, the broad. I think he does too. It's just the hollowed-out main floor of a house. That's all it is."

"They don't just jump gavachos for laughs, do they?"

Murray shrugged. "About anywhere's else I could tell you. But Whitefence..."

And that's what it was—a white fence, stretching for a solid block along Whittier Boulevard, hiding the hollow below. I told the cabbie to go down Bernal, and we took a fast ride through Whitefence. Murray's briefing made it familiar to me—except for the people. They all seemed to be cut from the same mold— full, sweeping heads of glossy, black hair; compact bodies wearing khakis or denims, T-shirts or jackets. And whatever else they wore, the shoes were universally objects of admiration.

"Make a right at Euclid," I told my driver. "Go down to fourth and up Fresno."

He nodded, got into the right lane. A clanging R car slid up alongside us at the light. Everywhere were the black eyes, impassive faces. Girls in bright, bright dresses on their incredibly trim bodies added color to the drabness. They looked light; they looked ready.

We turned up Fresno. Houses pushed one another, most of them unpainted. Children ran about. We came to the corner where El Encanto stood. Murray had been right—there was no street sign on the corner. A tough-looking group of young Mexicans loitered in front of the joint. We approached it almost head-on coming down Fresno, although the door was on the other, the unnamed, street. It was just a bar with a dark hole for a door, and tin signs in both English and Spanish tacked about. A blue neon hung over the door with the name gleaming uselessly in the pure light of three o'clock.

"Turn left here," I said.

The driver whipped the slow-moving yellow cab around into the unnamed street. My eyes stayed with the El Encanto as we passed. He was in there. Robert Vellardo…Huero. My lips burned for some funny reason and it felt like someone was pulling separate veins out through my fingertips. We came to Bernal and the driver asked: "Which way here, Mac?"

"Right. Up to Whittier."

"Say, Mac," the driver said. "Like I know, it's none of my business." He turned down Whittier Boulevard, drifted with the increased traffic. "But what the hell're you looking for?"

"An honest man," I said, straight-faced.

He made a sound with his lips. "Okay, so where to now?"

I had him let me off at Boyle, paid him. I made a call to Maggie from a chain drugstore on the corner. Murray and Bootnose and four others would meet me at the El Encanto as soon as they could get there. Maggie was to give them carfare.

Now I needed a car, and maybe a driver. I began walking, and then I found what I wanted on one of the quiet residential streets off Boyle. He was a sharp kid, about twenty, well-built and well-shod like the rest. He had the hood off a '41 Mercury re-built that had five inches of windshield and not a piece of chrome on its smooth, uncluttered, leaded body. Fender skirts were painted red; the rest was jet black. The boy was tinkering when I walked up. His T-shirt was spotted and grimy; the khaki pants had seen better days. But on his feet a pair of thick-soled, brushed-buck shoes gleamed in spotless elegance.

His black button eyes hit me when I walked up, flicked back to the screwdriver in his hand. I put my hands in my back pockets, watched. He went back to his tinkering. A rapid roll of Spanish spattered the quiet. The boy raised his head, answered shortly. A woman stood on the steps of the house behind me. I nodded politely and she turned away. The boy finally came out of the engine. He wiped his hands carefully, spread-fingered, on the front of his trousers. His face was impassive.

"You looking for something, man?" His English was without accent except for a slight rising inflection.

I shook my head, nodded unsmilingly at the car. He turned; we both looked. After a time he said, "It's an iron, huh?"

I agreed without speaking.

"You like it, man?"

I nodded again and walked all the way around the car. It reflected hours of patient work and dedication. I still said nothing. The boy, some of the tight control leaving his features, pointed into the engine compartment.

"That's a fifty-five. Had to re-mount the blocks and set it a little on a bias. Then it wouldn't clear the Bell Housing by a hair so I leaned the radiator and bent the fan blades back a little." He motioned. "See here? The way they go?"

"Yeah," I said. "Cooling system all right?"

"Oh, yeah. Don't bother it at all. And you know what? It improves the high-speed performance." His eyes blinked with concentration. "The only thing is, I didn't chop it and do the channeling myself. Another cat did it and I don't like it. But I got it cheap."

"What kind of cam?"

He looked at me like I'd asked if Marilyn Monroe was a girl. "An Essegian," he said. "Three-quarter race. My name's Moreno. Jimmy Moreno."

"Johnny Babcock. Like to go somewhere for a beer? Could you use one?"

Jimmy was a nice boy. An ex-soldier, Korea, he was finishing his education at Los Angeles City College and driving a truck for his father in the off hours. We got along fine. He liked jazz. I told him I played and we talked music. But it was getting late and I had no time to waste. The tavern we'd picked was full of music and Latin laughter and a mixture of Spanish and English that made me grin. Jimmy drank a beer and then, with the disconcerting shrewdness of his race, asked what I wanted. I told him—the whole thing, except the part about George Carter. But I told him everything about Huero. I had to. Money wouldn't make him help me and I needed him and his car badly. But the story won him—the story, the welt on my face and the fact that Huero was a Whitefencer.

"If he was just another chicano, why I wouldn't help you, man. You know?" His eyes, magnified by the gloom of the tavern, searched mine. "We stick together. We have to. But not with them Whitefencers."

He swore in Spanish, long and fluidly. I told him what I wanted to do. He agreed to go along, drive his bomb, and get us out of the hollow after we'd done what we set out to do.

"But it'll be tough, man. They even look sideways at chicanos they don't know. You'll have to walk into the joint with me. Keep your mouth shut. Then we grab the guy somehow, throw him in the iron and blow. But fast."

"It'll be tough, Jimmy. But I got to do it. I keep thinking of Darby up there on the thirteenth floor of the Hall of Justice, wondering if I'm going to help him."

"Sure," Jimmy said. His young face twisted with sympathy. "I wish you'd let me tell a few of the fellas. But if you say no, it's no. Now, here's what we'll do. ..."

CHAPTER EIGHTEEN

The motor didn't murmur, it growled. Even rolling in second gear over the bumpy, secondary road leading into Whitefence from Fourth Street, it snarled of power. The headlamps picked out debris and refuse; gates hung ajar, an occasional animal ran across the beams.

"What time is it, Johnny?" Jimmy's eyes clung to the twisting cart track.

"Seven-thirty."

Dusk had come quickly and now the headlights were necessary. This was the second time we had negotiated the road; the first had been to re-acquaint Jimmy with the twists and turns. Now we would fire for record. Murray and Bootnose and the rest were waiting in the vicinity of El Encanto. They'd be no help in a fight. You can't fight on wine. But they could confuse the issue, turn pursuers.

"Got the route marked?"

Jimmy nodded, tight-lipped. He had changed to a black nylon jacket and corduroys. The dash light turned his face olive with violet overtones.

He said, "Well, this is it"

"That's an original line."

"Yeah. Here's Fresno. The joint's right ahead. And look—twenty chicanos standing around outside."

"See anything of my friends?"

I looked myself. Then I saw Murray, Bootnose, and several others. They were spread around the three-corner intersection as inconspicuously as only the Brotherhood can loiter. Then we were there.

"Hope Huero doesn't recognize you," Jimmy muttered, pulling the Merc to the curb a little beyond the Encanto. "That scar's pretty wild."

"He won't. I had a beard, Jim. And I was a wreck. I'm heavier, now, and a whole hell of a lot cleaner."

We left the motor running. A small boy dashed by, spat words at us. The street had only a rudimentary sidewalk and it was peopled much too fully for my liking. But we were committed now. Jimmy walked confidently, with a sort of rock 'n roll swagger, toward the gleam of pale blue that spelled El Encanto. I followed, trying to look like a Mexican. Nobody bothered us. At the door, a ragged man approached me.

"Say, mister, you got a dime? Tienes un dime, señor?"

It was Bootnose. Jimmy cussed him out in Spanish for effect. The loungers laughed; but their eyes watched us, the strangers. I kept my head lowered, reached for my pocket. Bootnose moved close, his huge, blob-like nose mottled by the over-hanging neon.

He whined, "Un dime, no mas."

"Here," I said aloud. Then lower, "Get 'em all close. I'm going to snatch him quick as I see him. When you hear any commotion at all, go into your act."

I ducked inside. I don't know what I expected. But after all the nationalism I'd been subjected to, certainly not hot, constant modern jazz pouring from a Wurlitzer. That's what the Encanto was—a device to hold five hundred dollars' worth of music box.

A tiny bar sat at the right; behind it a piece of mirror reflected the drab room. No stools. Several mismatched tables surrounded the main object—a magnificent, gleaming new, one-hundred-play jukebox. The lighting was haphazard and low: one ceiling fixture with single bulb, and two wall brackets framing the piece of mirror on the backbar. A blue bulb burned over a doorway in the left rear.

The music drowned everything. A small, tidy man with a black mustache and white teeth stood behind the bar, a rapt expression on his face. Several men leaned on the bar, listening to the flow of highly amplified jazz. One girl—a tall, tightly dressed, dark-haired girl—hovered over the selection board of the juke. A light-skinned man with a slender body and a wild mop of hair stood beside her. One arm was draped possessively around her hip, the hand finger-spread on a rounded thigh. The couple's backs were to the door. But I recognized Huero. He'd shed the leather jacket. Tonight he wore a black shirt and grey slacks. And the blue suedes.

There was no undue attention paid to our entrance. One drinker nodded slightly at Jimmy. We elbowed the bar, waited for the mustache to pull himself out of the spell of the rubbery trombone-and-alto thing pouring from the speakers.

"Listen," Jimmy muttered. "I'll order. You nod."

"Okay." I nudged him. "That's the guy I want. The one by the box."

Jimmy turned, looked. The barman approached. His wet eyes were glazed, far away. I sniffed. The acrid odor of marijuana came to me. Jimmy ordered beer and the man went to get it.

I looked closely at the kid. His face was slicked with sweat and the black eyes moved constantly.

I said softly, "Take it easy, kid. It's only blood."

He grinned, shook his shoulders like a fighter. The bartender came back, slapped two red-labeled bottles in front of us. No glasses. I paid him with a limp dollar bill, evaded his wary, soft, tripping look.

"Johnny, if the motor dies, we're dead. We better do something."

I looked around. Huero and the girl had begun a low-voiced argument at the music box. The girl was facing him, both hands on her hips, pelvis stuck out defiantly. She rocked, haughty, contemptuous. Huero spat words at her. The record ended and his voice fell into the small bar sound. Suddenly he grabbed the girl's arm, jerked her. She pulled away, spit at him. Another record hit the needle. Trombones again. Huero twisted the girl's arm.

"Jimmy," I said. "Get ready. I'm going to walk into that thing. Make it look like I'm protecting the girl or some funny thing. Got it?"

"I got it. Watch out for yourself. He's a cinch to have a fila—" He gestured, a cutting motion. "Belt him first, man. You walk him out, I'll cover."

I nodded, belly brick-tight. The room seemed awfully small and awfully full of people. But this was the man I had to have. As I reached the jukebox the girl squealed and swung a hand at Huero's face. He caught the swinging hand and twisted, turning the girl completely around. He pushed the arm up.

"Dirty bitch!" His eyes were mean, smoky and mean.

I said loudly, "Wait a minute, chum." I was almost close enough.

The girl whimpered and cursed in Spanish. Huero's eyes returned to her. He jerked the arm cruelly high. She screamed, jumped to escape the pain. Her body curved out and her fine legs buckled.

Huero said. "Get lost, man." He spat the words at me, flecking the girl's coal-dark hair with saliva.

The girl, hurt beyond endurance, howled and twisted. Huero wrestled with her, and I circled to get a good shot at him. His eyes flashed at me over the girl's bouncing head. Suddenly he stopped.

"Hey! I know you. That face…"

Behind me I heard a crash. At that moment the girl flung her head back, cracking Huero flush on the nose. Tears leaped into his eyes, and he held his nose, backing away. I braced my feet wide on the slick floor for leverage, brought a punch up from way down. The skin on my knuckles split on his teeth. The slim body flipped, slammed against the juke.

"Watch it, Johnny!"

Jimmy's cry saved my life. I wheeled. The bartender, fist full of glittering knife, scrambled at me.

"Watch the blade!" Jimmy hollered from near the door, holding a man in his arms.

The mustache came at me silently. He moved in, weaved. I dipped a knee to the left, started a right hand. The guy flinched away and began a vicious stab from low down, right at my belly. I fell away to the right, the blade whistling between my left arm and my body. At the same time I lifted my knee to his groin. He was stepping in, following his thrust. The knee ruined him, and he bent over, making funny sounds with wide open lips. I swung the split knuckles from my hip pocket and hit him flush on the open mouth. It made a sound like two wet logs slapping together.

Then things got all mixed up.

Someone yelled. "All right, Johnny!" A bunch of ragged men milled at the door. The tough Mexicans, who had been standing out front as we came in, tried to get through the door. No one had any idea what was going on.

"Go, Johnny," Bootnose said, materializing beside me. There was a cut on his face. "Hurry," he said.

I ran to Huero. He hadn't moved. His face was a mess and he was cold. The fight raged all around me. But nobody seemed to know who was fighting whom. It was more like a mob scene for a cheap movie. I picked the slender Mexican up from the floor and muscled him over my shoulder in a rough fireman's carry.

Jimmy ran to me, wiping a streaming nose. "Let's go, man," he said. Now he was really grinning. The White-fencers would have some wounds to lick. "The door's clear," he said and led the way.

We started through the mess. A yelling Mexican reeled against me, threw me off balance. Jimmy spun the man, hit him in the belly. Bootnose came roaring across the floor, hit a knot of struggling men near the door. Just as I got to the door, I saw Murray Altrock, a beatific expression on his face, holding tightly to the tall brunette. She was crying and tossing her head; Murray came up to her nipples. He waved at me and said something I didn't catch.

I made it outside and ran to the car. Huero's hanging limbs banged against me.

"Hurry up," Jimmy said, and opened the car door. "Here they come."

"I'll throw him in back. Get the wheel and let's get out of here."

I dumped Huero into the back seat. The motor roared. As I started to slide in, a weight landed on my back. A fist-waving youth climbed all over me from behind. I turned partially, grabbed the door and slammed it on the Mexican. The edge struck him under the arm. He howled and let go of my neck. I stepped out into the street, grabbed the guy. He swung and I ducked, then popped him with a straight right as I came up. He fell away. A knot of man-shapes broke away from the Encanto's door rushed toward the car.

"Let's go, Jim!"

"Check, man."

The motor revved and the gears sang. We fishtailed out of there. I don't know how Jimmy straightened in time to make the left turn at Orme. But he did. Then we were rolling. Over the Merc's howl I heard another motor spin into life.

"Watch behind, Johnny."

"Got it. Just get—"

A police car came at us around the corner of Bernal. Jimmy burned rubber to keep from hitting it. There was no other traffic. Cops' heads turned as we passed, rounding the corner onto Bernal. Then we had it made. A straight run for the dirt alley— our escape hatch.

We passed the street the Encanto was on, the length of the block away. Only a few figures now. A car's lights came on, turned up the way we had left. At that moment the Merc lurched, slid, swayed in a high-speed turn. The tires protested as Jimmy bent the car into the tiny alley opening between two ramshackle buildings.

"This is fine, man," Jimmy muttered.

The wheels spun. We hit an open gate, sent it screaming through the night. A terrified pair of eyes, whether human or animal I'll never know, loomed off to the left, were gone in a flash.

"Anything behind?"

"Nothing." I shifted on the seat, forgetting the front. That was up to Jimmy. He knew the way.

But there was action behind. A light showed in the winding road, but still far back. I said nothing to Jimmy—the Mercury was flying now as it was. A siren growled back where we'd come from and I knelt on the seat, peering through the slit of the cut-down back window. No flashing red light. Not yet. On the floor of the back seat lay Huero, flopping with the motion of the car. I must have really hit him.

"How far?"

"Pretty quick," Jimmy said. He slowed suddenly. "Look ahead."

A street, filled with lights of moving traffic, seemed to leap at us.

"Fourth," Jimmy yelled, and babied the wheel, sending us around a stack of boards that could have been a house. "Watch it!"

And before I had time to be scared, or duck, we had zoomed right at the traffic-laden street, flashed under it. The clearance couldn't have been more than three inches. A regular car would never have made it. We slowed further. Jimmy flipped off the lights.

"Where are we?"

"Gleason," he said, never taking his eyes from the badly lighted street into which we had turned.

It was houses. And stores. People all over the place. Then we turned again. This time the street was a busy one, with streetlights and much traffic. Jimmy used the headlights again. We wove in and out, moving just a bit faster than the law would allow.

"Lorina," Jimmy said. He grinned. "We got it made now, man. We beat 'em, by God! Snatched Huero right out of Whitefence. I got a story for the fellas."

"You sure have, kid. And I've got one to get—for the police."

Behind us the siren sound diminished, faded out altogether. We drove into the city night, saying nothing, feeling the close kinship of hunters after a successful foray. I leaned back, lit smokes for both of us. A clock on a jewelry store said nine-five.

I listened for a moment at the door of the apartment. A murmur of conversation came to me. Dee's voice and one other. I gripped the knob, turned it. The voices stopped and full room lighting hit me in the face. I stepped inside, blinked. Albert Freese's voice said, "I never did want to sell you that policy, Babcock."

"I remember," I said. "I wish you hadn't."

"Johnny," Dee said. Just my name. Her hand was at her throat; her eyes, deep and liquid, stared at me. Then she got her tongue unstuck. "Did you—Is he—"

"Relax," I said.

Relief swept her face and it almost made me laugh. She closed her eyes, leaned back. I moved to the couch, sat beside her.

Freese said, "I've been listening to a rather incredible tale, Babcock." His wise eyes lifted to my face, traced the scar, the lines at eyes and mouth corners. "You look like it might have a little merit."

"It has."

Dee said, "I told you, Mr. Freese. Johnny's been trying to get the mess straightened out. But now he needs help. We came to you because there is no one else. He's supposed to be dead."

Freese sucked at his pipe; it whistled emptily. He took it out of his mouth.

"Yes, I know. Dead a hundred thousand dollars' worth." He leaned forward. "I want that money, Babcock. I want that understood—clearly understood."

I nodded, tired now that the excitement was over for a while. I felt Dee's hand slide inside my arm.

"You'll get it," she said quietly. "If Edna's spent it all, we'll make it up. Johnny and I. No matter how long it takes."

"Well, now that's nice. But I'm afraid the law is going to have some small say about what happens. I don't want you to get the idea I'm buying your story. I'm not. It still looks to me like a plot was laid to bilk my company." He settled back, brushed an ash from the grey suit. He crossed his legs. "But I'll listen to whatever Babcock has to say. It's a weird affair, at the least. But I'm interested enough in the possibility of recovery—even partial recovery—to give the benefit of every doubt."

"That's all I ask, sir." I sat on the edge of the couch, pulled away from Dee. "When I'm through, I hope you'll see that what happened was—"

"Just a minute," Freese said, cutting me off. "Before you go too far, let me get this in. This young lady has espoused your cause at great length. It hasn't been entirely unpleasant. Good company, good liquor. We've talked for—" he glanced at his watch— "some three hours. She's told me quite a lot of interesting things. One thing, however, she hasn't touched upon."

"What is it?"

He stuck the dead pipe in his mouth, held my eyes with his narrowed ones.

"The body in the canyon. Who is it? How did it get there? And who did it?"

I nodded, wet my lips. Dee curled up at the end of the couch. I talked.

CHAPTER NINETEEN

"You don't look very well at all in this, Babcock," Freese said. The insurance man leaned forward in the chair, laid his cold pipe on the coffee table. The wall clock said ten minutes after ten. I had talked for almost an hour. Dee rose, took the glasses to the kitchen.

"You say," Freese continued, settling back, "that you did indeed intend to defraud Mercury-Consolidated. That you did in fact plan to do away with George Carter."

"Yes, sir. There's no way to soften it. That's the way it was. But I didn't kill him."

"And you expect me to help you escape the consequences of your act?"

There it was. That's how it looked to him—how it would look to anyone. Anyone who didn't know Edna.

"No, Mr. Freese, I don't." I rose abruptly and paced to the window. The night was grey, filled with eye-burning smog. Haloed lights showed through like low-hanging nebulae. "Not escape. I don't deserve to escape entirely.

I wheeled, walked toward the big man in the chair. "But neither do I deserve to die for being a fool. I do deserve some consideration for calling you, giving you a chance to make full recovery of the money. I could have gone to the police."

"Why didn't you?"

"Because I can't prove I didn't kill George Carter. And that's what I must do. Right now, at this moment, I can't prove it. That I wasn't near when it happened. And that's the whole point. You see, I know I would never have had the guts to go through with it. But my knowing it is not enough."

"It isn't," Freese agreed. He glanced toward the kitchen where Dee, making drinks, was clinking glasses. "But look here, how can you get Edna to admit that she killed him? I've had dealings with this woman. She hard and she's smart."

"I know." I sat down again, ran my hand through my hair. "I know. Believe me, I know. And she knows it, too. If I holler cop, even now with this Robert Vellardo in my hands, she can sit tight and get out with a jail sentence."

"While you take the big trip."

"That's right. That's why I need your help."

His eyes slitted at the mention of help. He picked up his pipe, began filling it again. I reached for a cigarette.

"She's hard and she's shrewd, Edna is. She knows there were only two people on that mountain top. She knows that with the trail I left, I'll be the one held responsible for the crime. Okay." I paused, lit the cigarette. "She won't panic. She's not the type. I have to use a lever, and it has to be a good one. The only slip she's made was trying to have me killed. There was no need for that. She knew I couldn't go to the cops. But she was afraid that in my hopelessness, I'd fall afoul of the law in some ridiculous way and lead the police to her. She wouldn't die for the murder—but she'd lose that money."

"What a story."

"Yes. That's the way it is. You see, if I can get this kid Vellardo—Huero—to scare, he'll run to Edna. She'll have to do something. When she does, I'll be ready."

"So you'll make a clay pigeon out of yourself."

"What other choice have I?"

"You could run."

"Yes, I could. And that's all I'd ever do. No thanks. I've had a taste of being Mr. Nobody from Nowhere. You can't imagine how that is. So I'm going to clean it up right."

"That means doing some time."

"I know." Dee walked up behind me silently, put a hand on my shoulder. I smiled up at her, turned back to Freese. "That's the way it's got to be."

I leaned back. Freese sat there puffing slowly on his briar. His eyes stared out the front window at the haze. Nobody said anything. Dee brought the tray of drinks around, set it on the table.

The big man let out his breath in a long sigh. He sat up. "All right. I'll do it. And I'm breaking the law." He smiled at Dee, a little ruefully. "This is a woman, Babcock. She talked a hole in my head before you came. She must love you very much."

There was a knock on the door. I jumped up, opened it. Jimmy Moreno stood there blinking in the rush of light.

"You said ten-thirty, Johnny. Here he is."

He pulled Huero into sight. The bridge of the slim man's nose was crusted with blood; both lips were fat, shiny. His face was sullen and the mean eyes were hooded.

"Bring him in."

Freese had his coat on when we got the skinny kid into the living room.

"I'd better be going," the insurance man said. He looked at Robert Vellardo, shook his head. "Only a boy."

"But a bad one. Look at this scar." I touched my face where the chain had left its imprint.

"Yes. I guess so." He walked to the door. Dee went with him. "I'll make the call from a nearby drugstore. It'll take about an hour. Maybe an hour and a half. All right?"

"Fine. Dee, go with him to his car, huh? And take your time."

After they left, Jimmy pulled Vellardo into a chair and twisted his hands behind him. Huero. His skin was very light for a Mexican and his eyes were dark blue rather than the absolute black of most Mexicans' eyes. He spat a string of curses and Jimmy tugged on his arms, pulling them up his back.

"Keep your tongue, pachuco. You been lucky so far."

I got a robe belt from the closet and tied Huero's arms behind the chair. Then I went around in front of him, stood there where he had to look at me.

"Remember me, Huero?" He dropped his head, mumbled something. "Look at me, punk! Look at the scar. See it?"

"Don't tell me your troubles, gavacho," he said. His head swung from side to side, bushy hair swishing. "You better let me go, man. I could sue you."

Jimmy, behind him, grabbed a fistful of hair and slammed the glossy head back against the chair. Huero's eyes filled and his mouth sucked in.

"You listen to me, sucker," I said, very low, very hot. "Listen good. I got no time to be gentle. I want to hear about the woman that hired you to kill me. I want to hear all about it. How it came about, where you met the woman, how much she paid you— every damn thing."

He didn't want to tell it, of course. Jimmy was more impatient than I. He belted Huero a couple of times but the kid had guts of a sort. He was hurt, but he wouldn't talk. Dee came back, and her presence dampened the questioning. Vellardo sensed it and clammed. After a fruitless half-hour, Jimmy called me into the kitchen.

"Look, Johnny, I'm hip to this kind. He's never gonna talk now. Even if we bang on him. He knows he stands a chance of going to the joint if the fuzz find out about his part in the killing. You know?"

"Yeah, I know. But I've got to get him to sing, Jim. I've got to!"

"Why? You know who hired him."

"Yes, but I've got to get him to say it in front of witnesses. Then he'll go to Edna."

"All right," Jimmy said, moving close and lowering his voice. "Listen to me…"

Dee was wiping the kid's face with a wet towel when we got back. He face was a study in conflicting emotions.

"Do you have to get rough, Johnny?"

I sighed. "No, Dee. I don't have to get rough. Unless I want to stay out of that little green room upstate. And I do."

Jimmy came behind me carrying a bunch of equipment—wires, a box and bright pieces of metal.

"Where to put this stuff, Johnny?"

"On the table. Hook it up and turn it up—way up." I turned. "Now, Huero, here's the sketch. You and me are going to play a little game."

"I ain't got nothin' to say, man. I told you that. I ain't done nothin'. I ain't sayin' nothin'." His eyes found Dee; a smug look came over his bloody features. "And you better let me go, gavacho. I'll sue your ass off..."

I bent and pulled one of his legs back alongside the chair. His beautiful blue suede toe scraped the carpet.

"Hey!"

I moved around, got the other leg. "Like I said," I muttered. "We play quiz show. I ask, you answer."

He hollered. First in English, then in Spanish. I had hooked his toes over the side rung of the chair on each side, pulled his hips forward on the seat. He hung there. stretched wide open, held by his strapped arms, his knees pointed toward the floor. His lip trembled and he bit it.

"Wait, now. Wait."

I turned away from him. Jimmy fussed with the stuff on the table. A dial gleamed from the pile of equipment; Huero's eyes found it. Jimmy kept his head away to hide a grin. He knew his people.

"What're you gonna do, man? What're you gonna do?" He spouted the same question to Jimmy in their language.

Jimmy shrugged, pulled a long face. He answered him shortly. I heard "Su huevos," and walked up to the chair. His face had gone grey. I pushed the taut thighs further apart. He squirmed, seemed to draw within himself. His eyes were wild.

"You wouldn't," he said, hardly getting it out.

"Wrong. I would. Jimmy, turn the recorder up to full volume. We want to get it all." I saw Dee start at those words. She knew we had no recorder. "All right, hard guy. Here it is, the rules of the game. I'm going to ask you questions. Every time you don't answer, or tell what I think is a lie—boom! I kick. Right where you live."

Dee stuck a fist in her mouth. The kid in the chair almost died. But I didn't have to kick him. He opened up like a burst hose. Actually he didn't know a hell of a lot and what he did know was no good for my purpose. But he spewed. About how Eddie Samuels had approached him with a proposition for beating up a guy for this broad he knew. The broad's name was Babcock. I made him repeat it. He was sure of it; he swore to it. That's what I really wanted. His admission. And I wanted him to believe that every word was being recorded. Jimmy had told me that Mexicans have an inordinate fear of things mechanical; they make oracles out of radios, gods out of lie detectors.

"All right," I said, when he'd said enough for my purpose. "That'll do it. Jimmy, take the recorder in the other room. Lock it up."

Jimmy said, "Aren't you going to call the cops?"

"Tomorrow. Lieutenant Dembrun isn't on and I have to take it to him. First thing in the morning, we'll go to the Hall of Justice."

"You mean we gotta sit up all night?"

"It's almost midnight. Not so long."

Dee had been pulling on my arm since the questioning ended. I frowned at her, hoped she wouldn't say something wrong. I pushed her towards the kitchen.

"Go fry me an egg," I said. "I'm starved. Haven't had a bite since a sandwich at three o'clock." She hesitated, eyeing me very suspiciously. "Go ahead." I patted her.

Jimmy came from the bedroom. He nodded.

"Watch him, Jim. I'm going to grab a bite."

I ducked into the kitchen.

Dee said, "Johnny, what are you doing?"

I grabbed her. "Shhh. Jimmy's going to set that guy loose. Make some noise. Rattle some pans."

She didn't argue. At the stove she banged a skillet, slid a pan over the grates. Then she turned to me.

"Johnny..."

"Yes." I came away from the door. Jimmy and Huero were whispering in Spanish.

"Could you have done it? Kicked him, I mean."

"I don't know, Dee. It was Jimmy's idea. And it worked. I don't know if I could have gone through with it or not."

"I don't think you could," she said. She wrinkled her fine eyes.

A faint murmur came from the other room.

"He's turning him loose."

"Why, Johnny? What—"

"Listen, Dee. This junk is no good. What I need is an admission from Edna about George Carter. That's all I care about. And I'd like to have it on a real tape recorder. Not a transistor radio and a length of electric cord from a mixer."

"I wondered about that."

I grinned at her, rubbed my face. "Freese gave me the idea. Now, you listen. There's no time for jazzing around. I want to wrap this up tonight."

"Oh, Johnny, I hope so." Her eyes filled, and I pulled her to me. Her words came muffled. "I love you so much. But I'm so tired of this—this hassle!"

"So am I. But it won't be long. Listen..."

I kissed her quickly, tilted her head back and told her what she had to do.

"Jimmy'll take you to a hotel. Now you get a room, stay in it. You can't help me now. No one can. Heuro should run right to Edna. She has to move, thinking I'm going to the police. I'm hoping she moves in my direction."

"Johnny, let me call Rudy. You can't do it alone. What if she brings somebody?"

"Who? Vellardo?" I laughed, patted her back. "No. Don't call Rudy. Understand?" I let her go and walked to the sink, rested my hands upon it. "This is something I have to do myself. There comes a time when a man has to know he is a man."

In the other room there was a scuffle. A sound, like somebody falling to the floor. Jimmy cried out and footsteps raced across the apartment.

I hollered, "What's going on out there?" and fumbled with the kitchen door.

When we got there, Robert Vellardo—Huero—had gone.

The door to the hall was open. Jimmy sat on the floor trying to keep from laughing.

"He went for it, Johnny. Like a ton of tortillas," Jimmy got up, dusted his cords. His hair was mussed. "I told him I'd cut him loose if he got a hundred bucks by noon tomorrow and met me at the Encanto. He said okay, then, when I untied him, he belted me and ran."

"Good, Jimmy, fine." I walked to the youth, took his square, strong hand in mine. "I don't know what I'd have done without you."

"Aw, man ..." his eyes slid away; he shrugged. "It was kicks, you know?" He pulled away, turned to Dee. "Let's go, Miss Dee. It's past my bed time."

Dee walked up to him, stared at his face for what seemed a long time. Color climbed in his cheeks. His nose was swollen slightly and there was a small cut under one eye. Her fingers touched his wounds fleetingly. Then she raised on tiptoe and kissed him. Jimmy looked like he wanted to jump out the window.

"Thanks for helping him, Jimmy. When all this is over you'll be a favored guest at our house ..."

"On West Anniversary Drive," I put in.

The man came ten minutes after Dee and Jimmy had gone. I opened the door to his knock, let him in. Freese must have broken a few speed records.

"You Mr. Babcock?"

"Yes. Come in."

"Albert Freese sent me," he said. He set two leather cases on the floor gently. "I got a man out in the car. I'm Winslow. National Protective. We contract investigation for Merc-Con."

I shook his hand into the room. He was a little man with an almost totally bald head and droopy chins. He was about forty, short-legged and weary-looking; a rumpled suit hung on him like a sack. He certainly didn't look like either a detective or an electronics expert.

"Drink over there if you want it. We haven't got much time, Mr. Winslow."

He walked toward the bedroom, peered in. Then he went to the front window. "This overlooks the street?"

I told him it did and mixed a pair of drinks. Mine, I loaded. It was to last me for a long time. Then I took a bottle and a quart of mix into the bedroom, returned for Winslow's cases. They were heavy. Recording equipment usually is. The little man was going over the living room intently, looking, he said, for a place to put his mike.

When I had set up the bedroom to my liking I went back to the main room and found Winslow on his knees by the couch.

"Find a place?"

He grunted, got up. "This lamp ..." He picked up a modern triangle-and-knob thing from the end table. "You mind if I drill a little hole in it? And in the table? Just tiny ones."

"Drill anything," I told him. "And chop anything. What I want is a record of every word that's said in this room. Freese tell you about it?"

"Just enough. What's the pitch?"

I told him briefly. I wanted to enlist his sympathy, if possible. Along with his knowledge. When I'd finished, he grunted. His face betrayed nothing. But he said if a mouse walked barefoot across a pound of cotton in the room, he would record the footsteps on his Ampex. I believed him.

"This is for you," he said. He had a pistol in his hand. "Go ahead. Take it. Freese told me to bring one, give it to you. Evidently he thought you might need it."

I hefted the gun. It was a .38 police positive. Ugly. Very efficient-looking. I didn't think I'd need it for Edna, but I stuck it in my coat pocket.

Winslow asked me to get his partner from the car while he set up for recording.

"Why? Can't you do the job alone? I'd like to have it as nearly natural around here as possible."

"Mr. Babcock, you want a record, right?"

"Yes, but—"

"You want it to stand up in court?"

"Of course."

"Then go get Pendleton." He turned for the bedroom, added over his shoulder, "Two witnesses. Get it?"

"I got it."

"And tell him to bring the auxiliary and the battery case."

"Battery case?"

The bald head twisted; he peered at me in the half-light of the room.

"Yes," he said, mouthing the words slowly. "Battery case. We can plug in the wall, yes. We can thus record, yes. But you're waiting for someone to try and do you in. Is that right."

"Look, I'm sorry I asked ..."

"Okay," he continued, as if I hadn't said anything. "People on the way to do other people in have been, in my experience, known to pull main switches." He squeezed both eyes shut, opened them quickly. "Main switch ... get it?"

A comedian. Three hundred private detectives in Los Angeles and I have to draw a comedian. Half-way down to the car I realized the byplay had been deliberate. He wanted me relaxed, capable of handling the situation. After all, if a murderer got by me there would be only one thin wall between him and death.

CHAPTER TWENTY

She came. Of course she came. The door was open slightly and the lights were low. I sat slumped in the big chair, sipping a drink. The only light was a swivel lamp I had turned to the door so that its pool spilled just inside where a visitor's legs would appear. The legs I saw were straight and slim and would sell anybody's hosiery. She stopped right there.

"Johnny…"

Her voice was the same. It was as if we had never left West Anniversary Drive.

"Come in, Edna."

"You're expecting me?"

"Sure." I straightened a little in the chair. All I saw were legs, black high-heeled shoes and the very tip of a green coat. "Come on in. I'm alone."

She stepped in swiftly, pushed the door shut and leaned against it. Her face was shadowed. She wore a pulled-down hat like Marlene Dietrich, floppy and big-brimmed. The tie-belt of the coat pulled her body into silhouette against the light coloring of the door.

"I came to see you, Johnny. To make a deal."

I laughed. I couldn't help it.

"A deal, darling. Have I ever lied to you? Whatever you may think of me, you know I never lied."

"You never had to. Come on in and sit down. We'll talk. But I'll tell you I'm doubtful that we'll come to any agreement."

"Oh, we'll agree, Johnny… finally." She smiled. Her face was obscured in shadow, but I saw the smile.

"Where is your—What would you call her?" She moved forward, loosening the coat.

"Edna, stop it." I pressed my leg against the side of the chair where I'd put the gun. The lump was comforting. "You came to buy me or kill me. Get to it."

She walked quickly to the couch and stood there, eyes searching the room's shadows. I watched her like a poker dealer playing with Nick the Greek.

"You never could figure me, Johnny. Remember." She smiled; her tongue came out, ran over red, red lips. That same slow, knowing smile.

"I remember a lot of things. Sit down. Have a drink."

"No drink, thank you." She walked around behind me and I tightened. "What do you remember, lover? The nights when we made the world spin? The days when I called you at the office and you'd come rushing home? Those things. Johnny?"

It was hard not to turn, not to whip out the pistol and put an end once and for all to this sham. But I didn't turn or grab. Remembered fragrance drifted over my shoulder. I sat rigid in the dense quiet. Cool hands slid over my ears, lay flat against my temples. I felt Edna's breasts on the back of my head as she eased my head back, bent hers to look at me. Even upside down she was beautiful.

"I remember those things," I said, and my voice was without tremor. Her oval face, heavy with open lips, hovered over mine. Her eyes were murky. She moved her lips to mine in a slow, insinuating kiss, open-mouthed and full of fire. When she pulled them away I said, "I remember the mountain, Edna. George Carter—and the way he died."

She froze. Then she seemed to shrug without actually doing it. She straightened.

"Come sit down, Edna. Let's talk."

She hipped around to the couch, sat with her knees pointing at me, slim legs tucked a bit. Her eyes said nothing at all.

"You saw Huero. What did you think of his story?"

"Who's Huero?"

I ignored that. "But it doesn't matter. I'll make them believe me without him. And by them, kid, I mean the police. Cops. Fuzz. Nabs. You see, Edna, you made a bad mistake when you dragged someone else into it. Now I can tie you in solidly."

"You always could, darling. All you have to do is go to the police and I'm in trouble. You don't need poor Vellardo or anyone. Of course, when you do that, you die."

"You do know Huero?"

"Oh, of course. Let's not be childish. I came here to talk business. And don't tell me about your silly tape recording. I'm not interested."

I settled back, a grin working inside. She saw the ex-expression.

"You're not clever, Johnny. You're not—" She stopped suddenly, seemed to chew something over in her mind. Then she smiled again. "All right. With or without Huero you can have me put in jail. If that's what you want. We'll admit that and go on from there. What do you want—money? How much?"

"Not money."

"Then me. You want us to be together again. What's the matter, Johnny—isn't she as good as I was?"

"Leave her out of it." I shifted uncomfortably in the chair. I wished she'd take off that damn hat. "No, I don't want you. I want out from under that murder charge. That's what I want."

"Don't be silly. When George Carter died, no one saw the act. No one."

"Not even me. You knew I'd chicken out, didn't you? You figured that gentle Johnny, old lovable whisky-soaked Johnny wouldn't be able to go through with it."

"And I was right." She leaned back. "Where is all this getting us?"

Winslow could have told her. Winslow was getting every word. Get it all, Babcock. I told myself. I was filled with high excitement.

She spread the coat, untying the belt. Her dress was brown and very tight across the thigh. "The only thing you were ever any good for was bed, Johnny. You did all right there."

"Why didn't you just wait in the car? Then we wouldn't have all this. We'd still be together, I'd still have my job."

"And we'd still be broke. I pass."

"That's why you killed him. Johnny could chicken out but Edna would see to it that the money was paid." I got up and walked toward the lamp, stopped beside it. "The only mistake you made was in not killing me, too."

Edna sat quietly. Her hands lay relaxed and unmoving on her lap. Her lips held that secretive smile, like the whole world was nuts but her. I felt a cold shard of apprehension. This wasn't right. It wasn't going the way I'd planned at all. I was primed to cope with an avenging Edna, a threatening Edna; this act threw me.

"Maybe I should have," she said finally, nodding. "Maybe so."

I said, "You tried to remedy that with the goons at the Doniker. Almost got the job done, too."

"I had only a few tools to work with. After all, Johnny—" she swept off the hat, shook her hair— "I'm only a poor, weak woman. Remember?"

"Oh, I remember. Yes, ma'am, I do. I remember how George Carter's head looked. Like a muddy field after a parade. Weak woman. Oh, brother." I strode across the room, back to the table with the microphone. "You killed him."

"You can't prove that. And neither can anyone else. Why don't you come over her and talk." She patted the couch beside her. "I'll be generous. Johnny. Real generous."

"What if I can prove you did the actual killing? That I wasn't even near? What then?"

"Stop bluffing, Johnny. You can't prove a thing and you know it. No one saw me do it, and you were lying in your drunken stupor on the porch. You weren't near enough or smart enough to take a picture, so what proof could you have?" Her eyes flashed. "You weren't man enough to do it, but you'd never make a jury believe that."

I sank slowly into the big chair. My legs felt hollow, without fiber. I felt no triumph. Instead there was a great gaping hole that would take a long time to fill.

I said quietly, "That's it, Edna. Because now, I can prove you killed him."

My hand found the butt of the gun, gripped it. She made no move. The smile crept back to her lips; it hung, lazy and confident. Her tongue swept quickly over the lips. "That's interesting," she said. "Would you tell me how?"

"Throw your purse over here," I directed, lifting the .38 into sight. "Now. And do it careful."

"Johnny, do we need these melodramatics? I've—"

"The purse. And be careful."

She took the small evening purse in the tips of her fingers, threw it toward me daintily. It fell half-way between us. I didn't bother with it because it struck much too softly to hold a weapon.

"Satisfied?" She stretched, clenching her hands by her head. Her body jumped out in brown relief against the silk lining of her coat.

"Easy," I said, moving forward in the chair. "Real easy. I'm not taking any chances now that I've got what I wanted. Take off the coat."

"Oh, really, now …"

"Off, baby."

She shrugged out of the heavy green thing, pulled it out from under her. "Where do you want it, hero?"

"Edna, you don't seem to understand. You're treating this like some big joke."

"You are a joke, darling. You just don't think crooked." She laughed. "Your straight little mind is too busy worrying about the rights of others to plot successfully."

"You think so?"

"I know so." She leaned back. "You've taken my things. May I have a cigarette."

"No. You listen. All the while you've been talking, every word has been recorded."

It was quiet then. Real quiet. Her face didn't betray anything; she still seemed cool and assured. But that was her way.

"Did you hear me? Every word has been recorded. With witnesses. Now I can prove I didn't kill Carter. Now I can go to the police."

I watched for reaction; I wanted to see her break down. And she relaxed. I could see it. Like someone had just told her the dentist didn't have time for her. She sat back, the odd little smile returning.

"What's wrong with you? Answer me, damn it!"

"Johnny, you're funny."

"So I'm funny am I?"

"Yes. I don't believe a word of it, of course. It's a bluff. Like you pulled on that poor, young Mexican. But I'm not Vellardo, Johnny. You can't fool me."

I stood, gripping the .38. "I'll show you right now," I said. I walked to the table, bent over the lamp. "Winslow. Winslow, come on out. It's all over."

Her face changed then. But I couldn't read the expression. She should have been terrified. Instead the cold mask settled; she sat, watching.

"You're through, Edna. Done."

She didn't move, didn't speak. Winslow's voice came from the bedroom doorway.

"You know what you're doing, Babcock?"

"Yes," I said irritably. "Come on in. Bring Pendleton. Everything is fine. The job is done."

"You shake that crazy broad down for a gun?"

"Yes, yes." Something was still wrong. Wrong as hell. "She's not armed."

The little man advanced into the room. The headset hung from his neck dangled a length of rubber wire with a bright metal jack at the end. His expression was wary.

"We got it all. If that's what you just had to know."

"No, it isn't what I just had to know. I had to let her know it was done." I jammed the gun down into a side pocket and walked over to confront the silent woman. "I had to make her squirm."

"Johnny, you're ridiculous." She stirred, sat up. "Give me my purse. I'm getting out of here."

"Oh? Just that way, huh?"

"That's right, darling—just that way." She stood up, watching the bedroom door.

I said, "What's wrong with you? Don't you understand at all? You're going to go to the gas chamber. You! Not me."

"And you'll go to jail, Johnny."

"Yes. But not forever. And when I get out I'll have a good woman waiting for me. A good woman."

She smiled, bent for her coat. "I heard you."

Pendleton, a young, square-jawed man with sloping shoulders and a permanent squint, poked his head through the doorway.

"We done, Win?"

Winslow looked at me. I nodded, perplexed. Edna sat down on the arm of the couch. She lit a cigarette.

"Yeah," Winslow told the other man, "wrap it up. This is a screwy deal. I'm glad to be done."

Edna exhaled a cloud of grey smoke. "And hurry, please. I'd like to get out of here."

That did it. I grabbed her arm, jerked her upright. The cigarette dropped to the carpet, smoldered.

"You would, huh?" My teeth clicked together, and I could feel the bunches of muscles rising in my jaws. "Would you, now? Let me tell you something. When you leave here, doll, you leave with a cop on each side."

I tried to push down the surging anger, to control myself. "You hear, Edna? You hear?" I shook her. Just to erase that maddening smile, shake that magnificent assurance.

As usual, Edna knew what she was doing. She put her arms around me, pulled tight against me. I could feel every line of her. I thought she was going to kiss me; even now certain of her own physical appeal. But she was watching the bedroom door. The moment Pendleton walked through, she tightened her grip on me. I stood amazed.

Then she raised her voice, said in my ear. "All right, Sandy. Quick!"

I looked over Edna's shoulder. A man stood in the hall doorway holding a big automatic in one steady hand. The muzzle moved from side to side just enough to cover the room.

"Samuels!" I said.

He smiled. "You don't give anybody credit, do you, Johnny?"

"Oh, brother," Winslow said. He held the lamp with the mike like it was hot. "Oh, brother. I was afraid of this."

Pendleton said nothing, just stood, rooted with fascination, staring at the gun. Edna's arms stayed around me. I couldn't reach the gun. Then she began to slide one hand downward toward the pocket.

"You dirty bitch." I said it low and hot. Why should the piano player not want to be questioned about his brother? Why indeed? Because he had helped Edna, as some man always had, to cook up the scheme to get rid of me. Probably he had suggested his hoodlum brother for the job. He and Edna would get along. She had always been partial to the vital type.

"Now, Johnny," she said, and touched the gun through my pocket.

I moved, jerking her around in front of me. She bit my neck and I hoisted her feet off the floor. Samuels moved the gun muzzle, trying for a shot. I heaved and Edna let go; she spun over the couch, screaming. I thought of rushing the slim man who stood the length of the room away. I would never have made it, so I didn't try.

He stepped into the room, crouched. The gun was centered on me.

"Come on, Babcock," Samuels said. "One way or the other, you're gonna get it."

Then I started toward him. In the middle of the rush, I stopped, one leg bent, body inclined toward him. Pendleton and Winslow had not moved; Edna lay cursing behind the couch. Behind Sandy Samuels, the partially open door began opening wider.

"Come on, sucker," the man with the gun said, taunting me. "Come on. Hit me. Tackle me."

I froze. Rudy Dembrun slid through the door, advanced slowly. Samuels shook the gun at me.

"Come on, big man."

The Lieutenant had a gun of his own. He clutched it and moved forward, warning me with his eyes. His face was a dark, sharp wedge of concentration.

"Go ahead and shoot, Samuels," I said, barely getting the words out. I worried about Edna. If she came out from behind the couch... "Shoot, and be the second sucker to give up everything for that rotten woman."

Rudy Dembrun stopped behind Samuels. He reversed the gun, raised it. Edna screamed.

CHAPTER TWENTY-ONE

S AMUELS WHEELED and shot as Edna screamed. Wood jumped from the door, and a neat hole appeared. Rudy Dembrun flung himself forward, reversing his gun again. He fired and I heard the slug whistle past my ear. Samuels was untouched. They came together and grappled.

Edna hit me at the knees with her body as I started toward the struggling men. A gun went off. I twisted on the carpet, got a hand under Edna's chin, pulled her head back.

Dembrun and the piano player, each holding the other's gun hand wide, spun on the floor, grunting. They crashed into me and I lost the grip on Edna. She held on, sank her teeth into my leg. I raised the other foot, kicked down on her head. The pain in my leg lessened as the teeth pulled free.

Winslow cried out in the background. I saw Samuels rise from the floor, his hands empty. Dembrun rolled over and shook his head. He seemed dazed, but he still clutched his service pistol. The piano player hesitated. He could have gotten away while Rudy fought to regain his senses.

He dove for the fallen gun on the floor, came up with it and snapped a shot at me. It missed, hitting the little detective, Winslow, behind me. He let out his breath, sank to the floor. Dembrun came alive as Samuels aimed carefully.

I hollered as loud as I could, left the ground in a flying dive. It diverted the piano player. He fired, then the heavy boom of Dembrun's gun rang out. For the shadow of a second there was no sound. Samuels, a hurt, wondering expression on his handsome face, fell backward out the open door. The gun dropped from his fingers.

A figure flew over the body, ran across the room. It was Dee. She was crying and laughing and the room was in an uproar. Rudy stood in the center of the room, still crouched, his gun hanging from limp fingers. Pendleton knelt beside Winslow on the floor.

Dee plastered herself against me, rocking me back. "Oh, Johnny," she said, her wet face against my neck. "Everything will be all right, now. Everything."

I pushed her away. Edna sat up on the floor. Her dress had been ripped almost off. White thighs against red carpet in the low light. Her face was tear-streaked and a scratch ran down one creamy cheek. Not pretty. Not pretty at all.

Dembrun said, "Somebody turn on some light."

Dee, eyes watching my strange behavior, walked to the wall switch, put on the overhead cluster. The brighter illumination showed the extent of the damage. Winslow lay unmoving with the pale Pendleton hovering in attendance. Samuels was dead. Rudy checked his heartbeat, then stepped out into the hall and dispersed the excited and curious tenants of the other apartments.

Dee said, "Johnny…" and I walked away from her.

I looked down at the little detective on the floor.

"How is he?"

Winslow opened his eyes. "I'm all right," he said. "Upper leg. No bone. But no thanks to you, boy. You're a champ, you are. 'I'll handle it,' he says. 'Come on out, Winslow.' " He stifled a groan. "Yeah, you're a champ."

"I'm sorry," I said. My best line.

"You had to make her squirm, huh?" A spasm of pain took him and he closed his eyes, laid back.

"Take it easy, Matt," Pendleton said. "Easy. We'll have a doc here right away."

I turned away. Edna had pulled herself up onto the couch. She flopped there, arms over her head. I picked up her coat from the floor, threw it to her. Her bare legs offended me. Lieutenant Dembrun was on the phone to the police. He motioned to me.

"Get something and cover that thing in the hall," he said, then began speaking into the phone again.

A bunch of the morbidly curious had drifted back to stand with fascination over the remains of Sandy Samuels. I got a blanket from the bedroom, covered him. Then I walked to the window. Dee's eyes followed me everywhere I went. She said nothing. And I had nothing to say.

The city hung under the hazy night in gray blocks and shiny triangles of wet roof. I looked and looked but there were no answers there. Nearby houses showed lights here and there. All the noise, probably. Behind me, Rudy Dembrun, his small person embodying the authority of the city of Los Angeles, organized the remains of the battle. I heard him questioning Dee and the two private detectives, then Edna. He said nothing to me. Nobody said anything to me.

Edna came apart completely. I didn't watch. But I heard it all. She sat on the couch, wrapped in her green coat and the tattered remains of her once unassailable beauty, and told the incredible story of the past few months. Dembrun had Pendleton get it on tape. It would augment the admissions she had made to me. Dee came up behind me; I felt her presence but we did not touch.

"Johnny." Her breathless voice was subdued, uncertain. "Johnny?"

"Leave me alone, Dee."

"Rudy wants you," she said and walked away.

I turned. She had passed through the hall door, pushed past the chattering crowd of bathrobe-clad people clustered there. I wanted to call out to her, stop her. The words just wouldn't come.

"Babcock," Rudy said, "come over here."

"So now you know who I am," I said.

"I know. Sit down. Tomorrow morning the whole state will know. It's a big case. A hundred thousand dollars. Might even do me some good."

I sat on the big chair, dropped my head into my hands. It had been a long day. Edna sobbed quietly on the couch, muffled to the ears in her coat. Pendleton fiddled with the Ampex.

"All right. What do you want?"

"You had to play hero, didn't you? If Dee hadn't had enough sense to call me, you'd be cold meat right now."

"Maybe I'd be better off," I said dully. "I told her not to call you. I told her I could handle it. Hah! I handled it, all right."

"You're not a cop, Babcock." He lit a cigarette quickly, held it out to me. I took it. "I told you that before. You can't expect to do what you're not trained to do. Can I sell insurance, or steel? Or play piano?"

"How'd you know I played piano?"

"Dee. We talked quite a while about you. Now, look. I called homicide. They'll take a while, but they'll get here with the whole squad. When they do, you're going to jail. You know that?"

"I know it."

"And you're ready?"

"As I'll ever be. What will they charge me with?"

He blew out a cloud of blue smoke, studied the end of his cigarette. He sat single-haunched on the couch arm where he could keep an eye on the whole room.

"I don't know," he said, finally. "But with this stuff on the tape, I'd say accessory. Maybe conspiracy, if you're lucky."

"I'm not lucky."

"You're lucky," he said. "Lucky to have people like that Darby and the skid row boys. And Dee. Willing to go out of their way for you. Way out."

"All right. All right." I took a drag of the smoldering butt in my fingers, mashed it into an ashtray. "What was the thing with Samuels? I didn't figure him in this at all."

"Dee did. She knew from the first the connection between Edna and the two hired thugs had to be stronger than it seemed. When I told you about Sandy, out at the Chateau Beauvais, she had the whole play pegged."

"She didn't say anything to me."

"No. Of course she didn't. You were playing hero. Showing her, or yourself or somebody, that you could pull your own chestnuts out of the fire. But when you just ignored the piano player after the fight at the Domino, she knew you were in for a surprise. Perhaps a fatal one." He looked around, finally dropped his smoking cigarette end onto the carpet, stepped on it. "That's why she called me."

"I told her not to."

"Oh, for Christ's sake." He got up, walked to the window. "The squad'll be here pretty quick. You got anything to say, any talking to do, you better do it now."

"Will I make bail?"

"If you've got it. If you haven't, tell Dee to see me." He rubbed a hand over his eyes, looked quickly to the lifeless lump under the blanket blocking the doorway. "We'll get it up."

"How about Darby?"

"You'll see him. But he'll get out. No doubt about it. Your testimony, and Huero's, will spring him."

"Huero?"

"We'll get him. Now that we know the name. I called the report. Now, for Christ's sake, go talk to that girl, will you? You got a good one, and you ain't got sense enough to know it."

"All right," I said. I walked over to Edna. She looked up, eyes dull, face sallow and drained. She said nothing. She looked like a woman just out of the hospital after a long sickness. Only her sickness was just beginning. "Goodbye, Edna. I'll send you what you need. And some money."

She looked at me. Then she turned away. I walked out the door, through the crowd of curious people. They popped questions at me. I ignored them. My legs felt like cooked spaghetti; great weights dragged at my fingers. Through the glass of the front door I could see the outside steps. A lonely figure sat there, hunched, unmoving.

I walked out, sat down beside her. She didn't look up, didn't move. A siren wailed far down on Hill—coming here, in just a few minutes. The night was cool, now, and a faint breeze had blown the haze aside. Chipped ice floated in the dark sky and the city held its early morning breath.

"She still thinks I'm a slob," I said.

Dee nodded, face limned by a porch light from down the street. Her fine features were tight, controlled.

I said, "Maybe she's right."

"No, Johnny. You know she isn't." She turned her head. "What you have is a greater strength than any she is capable of evaluating. Think, Johnny. How many friends do you have? Good friends—friends who would do anything for you? I've noticed that from the very first. Remember Charley Dawson? The York Club?"

"Dee..."

"No. I want to talk about it. So it won't be between us always. I'm the woman for you, Johnny. I want you to know it, remember it. I called Rudy because I didn't want to risk losing you."

"How did you know about Samuels and Edna?"

"I watched him. That night at the Chateau. You were arguing with Edna. I watched Sandy Samuels at the piano. His face was very easy to read. I thought it funny at the time. But when he appeared at the Domino, threatened you, then I knew."

The siren got closer. It was climbing now. Soon the red light would blink around the corner and I'd be on my way to the square block of gray on Broadway—upstairs. high above the city. We sat together without words. Then Dee bent forward. She laid her head on her knees, looked up at me that way. I sat and looked at her and let the crimps work themselves out of my nerve ends.

"Johnny..."

"Yes, Dee?"

"I love you," she said. Her eyes closed and she hugged her knees. "I love you like crazy."

"Listen," I said, suddenly in a hurry, having much to say and no time to say it. "You know I love you. But I'm going to jail. I'll get out. On bail. They'll give me bail. There's still the house. Edna hadn't been able to sell it. Will you wait for me? We'll get married as soon as I get straightened out. All right, Dee? Will you..."

"If you go to prison, I'll wait." She said it quietly, with conviction and calm. "Married or not."

A police car howled around the corner, rocked to a stop in the street. Cops piled out. More cars pulled to the curb. A blinking red light brought a long, white ambulance to the spot. A young policeman, tall, with chevrons on his arm and a gun in his hand, ran up to us.

"This the place?"

I jerked a thumb over my shoulder. "Second floor, front, officer. Lots of shooting."

He started past, stopped. "What was it?"

I got up, pulled Dee to her feet and held her to me.

I said, "I don't know. Triangle, I think. You know how that is."

He swore. His young eyes swept over the horde of cops below on the sidewalk.

"Another Greeneye," he said. "Goddamn women!"

He ran up the steps and the rest followed. A stretcher went by, then a wicker basket. We stood on the steps, alone again.

"For a moment," I whispered.

She moved her hair against my face. "Longer to come, darling. All of our lives." She pulled back, looked up. The moon broke through at that moment and silvered the heart-shaped face, casting pools of shadow under the tilted eyes. "On West Anniversary Drive," she said, breathing it.

I kissed her. It had to last both of us for a while. We worked at it. When she pulled away my ears were roaring and her breath came loudly. Her face was flushed. Feet pounded on the stairs inside.

"They're coming for you," Dee said. "And I'm glad. Now maybe I can get some sleep."

THE END

www.ingramcontent.com/pod-product-compliance
Lightning Source LLC
Chambersburg PA
CBHW050837180626
46814CB00007B/2501